A CHANGE OF HEART

Abigail Norton's dream of owning her own beauty salon seems to be coming true when she finds the ideal location in a Merseyside village. But someone is determined to thwart her plans . . . Abbie can't help wondering if Tim Boardman, handsome owner of the travel agent premises next door, is trying to wreck her dream in order to expand his own property. When things take a more sinister turn, she wonders to whom she can turn for help . . .

Books by Karen Abbott
in the Linford Romance Library:

KAREN ABBOTT

A CHANGE OF HEART

Complete and Unabridged

LINFORD
Leicester

First published in Great Britain in 2007

First Linford Edition
published 2007

British Library CIP Data

Abbott, Karen
  A change of heart.—Large print ed.—
Linford romance library
  1. Love stories
  2. Large type books
  I. Title
  823.9'2 [F]

ISBN 978–1–84617–984–6

Published by
F. A. Thorpe (Publishing)
Anstey, Leicestershire

Set by Words & Graphics Ltd.
Anstey, Leicestershire
Printed and bound in Great Britain by
T. J. International Ltd., Padstow, Cornwall

This book is printed on acid-free paper

1

'Stop the car, Mark! It's over there!' she yelled as it came into sight suddenly.

'Don't do that, Abigail! There's a lorry close behind me!'

'And it's stepping on your tail!' Abbie chortled, not at all put out by her twin-brother's reprimand. 'Sorry, Mark! Couldn't help it! Only it looks ideal. Turn round at that roundabout ahead. We'll be on the same side of the road then and parking will be easier.'

She twisted round in the passenger seat, looking back over her shoulder at the *For Sale or Rent* notice board outside one of the properties on Church Road in the pretty Merseyside village. It was second from the right in a block of five, sandwiched in between a travel firm to the left and a flower shop to the right. The other two properties were a newsagent's and an orthodontist practice.

'In fact, if you're quick,' she continued, 'a car is just pulling out of the small pull-in space just outside it. For a village, the traffic's quite busy, isn't it? That means the shop will advertise itself, once I'm up and running!'

'If it's suitable,' Mark grunted. 'Don't go rushing in without considering all angles.'

Abigail screwed up her face at him, knowing the truth of his words.

'No, honestly! It will be ideal. I've got the details here. Listen, two-floored property for sale or rent with vacant possession. Downstairs, two rooms plus storage space; small cloakroom with WC and hand basin, space for a shower to be fitted. Upstairs, self-contained flat with independent access, comprising of living-room, bedroom, small fully-equipped kitchen and fully-fitted compact bathroom.'

'Just what I need. And the rental price is reasonable. I'm sure I'll get the option to buy after six months. That's what the bank manager suggested when I saw him.'

'Hmph!' Mark grunted again, his attention more on his manoeuvring to get the car into the recently vacated space than on his sister's enthusiastic words. 'Don't forget, I won't be here to help you out over the next few months, so don't take on anything you can't manage on your own.'

'We've been through all this, Mark! I appreciate all you do for me, but I want to stand on my own feet. Mum and Dad don't expect you to spend all your time looking after me just because they go away a lot.'

'I know. I just wish you weren't doing this right now whilst they're still on Dad's sabbatical in Germany. Still, I'll only be in America for four or five months. Then, at least, I'll be on the same side of the Atlantic Ocean as you. Anyway, out you get! Let's see what it's got to offer.'

Abigail scrambled out of the car and

looked up at the front of the building. The last owner had used the premises as a greengrocer's and remnants of his trade remained as a reminder. Faded notices offering apples reduced from 65p per kilo to 40p and a sack of potatoes for 99p still clung to the inside of the main window. Inside the main area, the shelves stood bare of produce, only a few price tickets and scraps of paper lay in untidy piles on the floor as if someone had started to clear everything away but had become disheartened part way through.

Mark joined her at the window, his hands cupped around his eyes to enable him to see better. 'It needs quite a bit of work doing on it,' he commented. 'Are you sure you can manage it? You can stay on in my flat while I'm away, you know.'

'I know, Mark . . . and thank you. You've been great letting me stay with you . . . but I need to start up again on my own.'

Mark's flat was in Bolton. It had

been her refuge for the past three weeks after the friend she had shared with had got married and Abigail had decided she needed a new start . . . both in her career and in where she lived. Too many memories lurked around in her previous place, so she hadn't taken up the option of renewing the lease in her own right.

Neither had she wanted to stay on in her previous job, where she was a beauty therapist at a thriving salon in the town centre. So, with a bravado she was far from feeling, she had handed in her notice and set herself the task of finding somewhere suitable for her to set up on her own.

Her face was aglow she turned to face her brother. 'And as to, 'Can I manage?', I'm quite sure I can, thank you! I've still got most of my share of Gran's money left. It should just about cover the necessary expenses. Oh, I've got such a good feeling about this, Mark. Let's dash back into St Helens and get the key. The estate agent said it would be available at about four o'clock, so we'll be just in time.'

The estate agent's office in town stood in one of the side streets off the Town Hall Square, which had recently been attractively pedestrianised. Mark parked as near as he could and strode after his sister, who, with success in her sights, was eager to further the process.

The girl on reception remembered Abigail from her previous visit. 'Ah, Miss Norton! Colin won't be long. He's talking to another client in the other room.' She nodded towards a door to her left. 'I'll let him know you're here.' She buzzed the intercom on her desk and spoke into the microphone. 'Miss Norton is back to see you, Colin . . . Pardon? . . . Oh! All right. I'll tell her.'

She switched off the machine and looked back at Abigail. 'Colin is taking another client who is interested in the same property to view it almost immediately. He says you may meet them there, if you wish.'

Abigail's face fell. She hadn't bargained on competition for the property. That might push the price up. She looked anxiously at Mark, glad now that he was with her.

'Don't worry,' he said, correctly interpreting her glance. 'You'll have the same chance as the other client. Don't let it push you into offering more than it's worth.'

The inner door opened and a middle-aged man stepped through, closely followed by Colin Jackson, the young manager of that particular branch.

Colin smiled a welcome to Abigail and Mark. 'You like the look of it, do you? I thought you would, from what you said you needed. Mr Sowerby, here, is interested in the property as well.'

The client looked very self-assured. His eyes glinted with confidence and something akin to superiority Abigail felt, instinctively disliking him. Sour by name and sour by nature! She forced herself to hold her head high and smile confidently as they exchanged brief formalities.

'We'll meet you there, then,' she smiled.

Mr Sowerby strode outside and Colin held the door open for Abigail to pass through.

'Sorry about this,' Colin apologised as she drew level with him. 'Mr Sowerby only came in this afternoon. Like you, he's only seen the premises from the outside.' He made a wry expression. 'He's rather keen, I'm afraid . . . both he and another client, a local businessman, who said he will meet us there this afternoon . . . but I'm sure we'll find you something else on the market before too long. It'll keep you brightening up my day for while longer, won't it?' he added with a mischievous grin, nudging her conspiratorially with his elbow.

Abigail tossed her hair back. 'He hasn't got it yet,' she pointed out sharply, refusing to be demoralised, 'and neither has the other man you mentioned!'

She noticed that Colin was finding it difficult to make steady eye-contact with her, as though he had already decided who was likely to buy the premises . . . and it clearly wasn't going to be her! She'd see about that!

They made the return trip almost in silence. Mark tried to keep Abigail calm and objective but he feared he was facing an unequal battle. That look was on her face! The one that had been prevalent in all their childhood squabbles and disagreements.

Abigail sat impatiently at his side, tossing all her options around in her head, hearing only faintly Mark's reassuring comments. She couldn't bear to be thwarted at this stage! She had set her heart on the premises. It was in an ideal position in a thriving large rural village a few miles north of the East Lancashire Road that linked Liverpool with Manchester.

Mr Sowerby nipped his car into the

only available space in front of the short row of shops. Abigail scowled at the satisfied expression on his face.

'Don't think you'll be beating me to the shop as well!' she muttered darkly.

Mark parked round the corner in Leyland Road. Abigail jumped out smartly and quickly made her way around the front again. Colin had already opened the door and was ushering Mr Sowerby inside.

'Yes, yes, just what I imagined it to be,' Mr Sowerby was saying, running his finger along the edge of the shelving and looking at it in distaste. 'Of course, it needs a great deal of work doing on it. It's a good thing I've got enough capital behind me. There'll be no problems there, Mr Jackson, I can assure you. How about you, Miss . . . er . . . ?'

'Norton,' Abbie said crisply, ignoring the inference that she would not have the needful cash so readily available. 'I'll have no problems on that score.'

She turned away and imagined the

front room made into a small reception area with a curved desk and some comfortable chairs for clients to sit on whilst they waited for their appointment.

She opened the far door and peeked into the storage room. It was larger than she had expected. Depending on what the rooms upstairs were like, it could have any number of uses. The small cloakroom and toilet led off from it and they, too, were satisfactory, though in need of sprucing up.

Mark had joined her and was nodding his head as he listened to her plans. She'd make a go of it, he was sure — if she got it!

'Of course, I can buy it outright,' Mr Sowerby was saying as they rejoined him and Colin. 'I just need to see the flat upstairs. If it's suitable for my manager to move into immediately, I think I can close the deal right here and now!'

Abigail's heart sank. There was no way she could compete with that. She couldn't even afford to buy it at all initially, not without a mortgage. She had been hoping to take up the rental option. She gripped hold of Mark's arm, appreciating his patting her hand reassuringly.

'Ah!' Colin looked discomfited, too. 'We have a small problem there,' he admitted. 'Nothing permanent or insurmountable,' he added hastily. 'As you know, there is a sitting tenant in the flat upstairs . . . but her lease expires soon.'

'That's no problem,' Mr Sowerby swiftly allowed, casting a magnanimous smile at Abigail. 'Shall we . . . ?' He gestured towards the external doorway that led up to the self-contained unit.

Abigail felt the bitterness of defeat. There was no way she could match his offer . . . and he knew it!

'However,' Colin continued, looking slightly fazed by Mr Sowerby's eagerness to close the deal. 'Mrs Crompton is in hospital at present and we have, just yesterday, agreed to extend her clearance date by three months to give her time to sort herself out. I'm sure she will do her utmost to leave as soon as she is able . . . maybe earlier than anticipated,' he added hopefully, seeing the look of annoyance on Mr Sowerby's face.

'Out of the question! It says here 'vacant possession'!' Mr Sowerby snapped, waving the details of the property under Colin's nose. 'You have been wasting my time, Mr Jackson!'

Abigail's hopes rose. She was sure they could reach some sort of compromise. She glanced at Mark. His eyes were guarded and he shook his head briefly, obviously warning her not to say anything yet. Abigail nodded and set her features into a non-committal expression.

'I'm very sorry, Mr Sowerby. Mrs Boardman's illness was unexpected and out of compassion for her age . . . '

'Away with your excuses! I haven't the time to listen to them!' Mr Sowerby said rudely. 'I have other properties to view . . . with other estate agents!

Good-day!' With a curt nod, he departed and they soon heard his car roar away.

Colin looked nonplussed by the speed of his exit. He brought his gaze back to Abigail. 'And you, Miss Norton? How do you stand?'

Abigail exchanged a satisfied glance with Mark. 'Oh, I think we might be able to come to some sort of agreement, Mr Jackson,' she smiled, 'especially since the other viewer you mentioned hasn't turned up.'

After a short discussion they returned to the estate agent's office in town and signed the necessary leasing document. Abbie felt well-satisfied by the deal she had struck with Colin Jackson on his client's behalf. She was initially going to rent the lower floor of the property for three months and convert the storage room into a temporary bed-sit.

If all went well, at the end of that time, or earlier if possible, if Mrs Crompton recovered sooner than anticipated, she would extend the rent to cover the whole property, with the option to buy after six months. Having been looking at suitable properties for over two months, she knew it was a sympathetic agreement on both sides.

Colin stood up and extended his hand across the desk. 'I think that covers all we need to do for the present, Miss Norton. It's been a pleasure doing business with you.'

As they turned to go, the outer door burst open and a dark-haired young man hurried in. He was dressed in a smart business suit. His hair was swept back from his face, revealing a sun-tan to die for.

Abigail felt an unbidden surge of interest in him, the intensity of which deepened when the man's smile included them in its warmth. His startlingly brilliant blue eyes seemed to burn deep within her. For a moment, it seemed as though time was standing still and she was struggling to bring herself back to reality even as he spoke.

'Sorry I'm late!' he apologised to

Colin waving his hand to indicate that he was willing to wait whilst Colin concluded his present business.

Colin's face fell. 'Mr Boardman! I'm sorry. When you didn't turn up earlier, I assumed you were no longer interested in the property. I'm afraid it is already let . . . to Miss Norton, here.'

A flash of annoyance extinguished the warmth in the man's eyes. 'Nonsense! Mr Yates knew I wanted those premises! I told him I would be away on business but he said he would give me first refusal when the lease came available! I've flown back as soon as my secretary told me! Where is he? We'll soon get this sorted out!'

'I'm afraid Mr Yates is on holiday, Mr Boardman,' Colin apologised, casting an anxious glance at Abigail, as if unsure where he stood on the matter.

'He left all his current transactions for me to deal with. There's nothing in his notes about you having any special interest in the place. If there were, I would have made sure that you were contacted before any other agreement was signed.'

Mr Boardman frowned. 'The agreement's signed?' He swivelled to face Abigail. 'You've bought the property, Miss . . . ?'

'Norton,' Colin quickly supplied.

'Miss Norton,' the man acknowledged curtly. 'What price have you offered? I'll offer you ten per cent more if you will re-sell the property to me immediately.'

Abigail gasped. Who did he think he was? Besides, she hadn't bought the place! Only rented it! But she wanted to buy it . . . later! He'd missed the deal, so tough luck! She wasn't going to back down that readily!

'I'm sorry, but that's not possible!' she said briskly. 'I want the property and the agreement is signed. Now, if you will excuse us, we have to go. I'll be in touch to get the keys in a few days, Colin. Goodbye for now. Come on, Mark.'

Abigail was in high spirits as they

drove back to Mark's flat in Bolton, the incident at the end pushed resolutely out of her mind and she insisted on treating Mark to a celebratory meal at Smithill's Hall, an old coaching inn on Chorley Old Road.

2

On Monday morning, Mark departed to America, satisfied that Abbie had everything in hand. Abbie didn't wait to watch his plane take-off. Mark travelled too frequently for such niceties. Instead, she excitedly restarted the engine of her bright red Fiesta and headed west on the East Lancashire Road, calling first at the estate office in St Helens.

Because she was renting initially, she was given permission to start on the work immediately.

Before starting work on the Tuesday morning, she decided to make herself known to the occupiers of the other three shops in the row and received a friendly welcome from the newsagents and Wendy, Liz and Moira, the girls in the flower shop.

'Time for a coffee break?' Wendy asked.

'Too right!'

'Good! Pop the kettle on, Liz. It won't be a tick!'

Wendy was the owner, Liz and Moira her assistants. They enjoyed a half hour's gossip as they got to know something about each other and all the girls promised to sample her services once she was up and running. Abbie felt greatly encouraged when she eventually sallied forth, expecting a similar reception from the travel agent's office.

However, the receptionist there was a different matter altogether. The young woman, in her late twenties, Abbie guessed, was immaculately dressed in a cream coloured suit, which showed off her auburn hair to perfection.

Her beautifully-manicured red polished nails poised over her keyboard as she arched her perfectly-shaped eyebrows.

'A beauty salon? Next door?' she queried, her highly cultured voice matching her supercilious expression.

'Are you sure? Tim hasn't said anything about it to me!'

Abbie felt rather under-dressed in her old jeans and baggy T-shirt.

'Who is Tim?' she felt compelled to ask.

'The owner . . . my boss. Well, he'll have something to say about that when he returns next week!'

'Why? What has he got against beauty salons?'

The receptionist's eyes narrowed. 'I don't think that is any of your business, Miss . . . '

'Norton. Abigail Norton.' She held out her hand. 'And you are?'

'Since we'll be having very little to do with each other, Miss Norton, my name is irrelevant. Now, if you don't mind, I have work to do.'

The receptionist pointedly returned her gaze to her computer screen and resumed her typing. Abbie made a wry expression and left, thinking what an unfriendly person the receptionist was, wondering how many holidays she managed to sell if she treated her clients in the same way.

When she glanced back into the shop as she shut the door, Abbie could see that the young woman was already on the telephone, no doubt reporting her presence to her boss . . . probably an elderly bachelor with Victorian views.

Abbie returned next door feeling slightly nettled. Then she shrugged. She would reserve full judgment until she had met the man himself. Surely he would be more approachable than his receptionist?

She gathered all the contents of the storeroom into the middle of the floor and set to work, brushing down the walls and ceilings; washing them down and then, after a break for lunch, applying the first coat of paint.

The following day, after informing Mark's neighbour that the flat would now be empty until Mark's return, she light-heartedly made the final journey from Bolton with her personal possessions.

Being a Sunday, she had expected the small parking area in front of the four shops to be empty. Instead, it was fully occupied. Hmm, with a car-full of possessions, she didn't want to park too far away.

As she paused, a customer left the newsagent's and went towards one of the parked cars.

Goody! That meant there would be space for her. She signalled her intention to turn right and slipped into first gear. As the other car began to pull away, the driver of a car coming from the opposite direction began to signal his intention to turn left . . . into her space!

'Oh, no, you don't!' Abbie muttered, determined not to have to carry armfuls of clothes from the next street.

She knew he had the right of way . . . but she was already signalling — and surely a gentleman would understand her predicament? Without thinking any more about it, she smartly continued her manoeuvre, nipping adroitly in front of him into the vacant space.

She switched off the engine and removed her key, felt under her seat for her handbag and turned to undo her door.

A tall male figure was standing by her offside wheel. His arms were folded in what she could only think of as a threatening manner and, as she bent her head slightly in order to see his face, his thunderous expression did nothing to make her feel any easier about him. It wasn't his expression that alarmed her the most . . . it was his identity!

It was Mr Boardman, the man who had wanted to buy her shop!

So, what did he want?

Did he intend to still try to wrest it from her?

Well, he couldn't! Colin had assured her that it was hers for at least the next six months . . . and she still had the option-to-buy clause. She had nothing to fear from the man.

Reassuring herself of that fact, Abbie thrust open her door and got out of the car and faced him with an outward show of boldness.

However, before she could speak, the man asked, 'Do you intend to spend the rest of your tenancy here thwarting me, Miss Norton?'

Abigail straightened her shoulders and ignored his question. 'You wish to speak to me about something, Mr Boardman?' she asked politely. 'Because, if you do, might I suggest that . . . '

'No. Until you drove recklessly in front of me in that high-handed way. I had no wish whatsoever to speak to you!'

'Then, why . . . ?'

'Why am I annoyed that you deliberately cut in front of me . . . into my parking space?' he asked with an undue amount of sarcasm. 'Is that what you were going to ask?'

She opened her mouth and then closed it again, her brain trying to make sense of what he had said. 'No . . . and what do you mean, into your space? It's no more your space than my space! And, since it's right outside my shop . . . ' She glanced at her parked car and its position relative to the row of shops. 'Or, nearly so,' she amended, 'I think I have every right to be there, especially since I have to unpack a lot of personal items! So, Mr Boardman, if you don't mind, I'd like to get on with it!'

'But, I do mind, Miss Norton . . . since you have parked exactly in front of my shop! And I also have a number of items to unpack!'

Abbie failed to understand. 'Your shop? It isn't your shop! It's mine! I got it first, remember?'

The man shook his head and pointed over her shoulder.

'That shop!'

Abbie turned to follow with her eyes the direction of his arm. He was pointing to the shop next to hers.

'The travel agent's?' she queried disbelievingly.

'Precisely!'

'But . . . ?' She was puzzled. 'If you already own the travel agent's, why go after my shop? It doesn't make sense.'

'It makes perfect sense!' he snapped, the blue of his eyes intensified by the inner fire of his annoyance. 'I had plans to extend. Plans that you scuppered! Now, if you don't mind moving your car, we can both get on with whatever we have to do!'

'I have no intention of moving my car!' she snapped back, determined not to be bullied by this arrogant man. 'You can see how full it is! It will take me ages if I have to keep locking the door and trekking to and fro!'

He looked . . . and what might have passed for a grin flitted briefly across his face.

'Good heavens! How much storage space have you got in that place? It'll need to be like the tardis to hold that lot!'

Hmm! He did have some vestige of humour, then! But Abbie wasn't sure

27

she wanted to see a human side of the man. She might get to feel guilty for beating him to the post! And she was aware of a warm tremor passing through her. Strange how his eyes suddenly lost the ice-cold sharpness; she felt almost mesmerised by the change . . . but sharply pulled herself together.

'Good management is all it needs! And I've got plenty of that!'

'I'm sure you have! Plenty of 'push and shove', anyway! Not that pushy females are my type! I prefer my women to be softly feminine.'

He seemed to throw her a challenging look as he coolly appraised her. Since Abbie was once again dressed in her oldest clothes, she knew she wasn't in the running for the best well-dressed woman award! Besides . . .

'Then, it's as well, I'm not your woman . . . nor ever likely to be, isn't it!' she snapped back. Really, the cheek of the man! Who did he think he was! 'And since we're being totally frank with each other, I like my men to be suave, yet warm-hearted . . . not arrogant, ill-mannered bullies who think they can bulldoze everyone out of the way!'

'Ha! Now we're getting down to it! Who bulldozed me out of the shop? And who bulldozed me out of my parking space? Tell me that, Miss Norton!'

'Yes, well. That was different. That was . . . self-preservation!'

Suddenly, the fight went out of her and she began to see the humorous side to their quarrel. Unexpectedly, she grinned.

'So, here we are, fighting like two quarrelsome children over whose game it is and who can or can't play! We seem to have got off to a wrong start, don't we? Shall we call it quits?'

'Typical of a female!' He cast his eyes heavenwards in exasperation. 'Since you're ahead on points, that probably seems to be a good decision to make!'

He was standing feet apart, the backs

of his hands on his slim hips . . . but what had started as an aggressive stance now seemed to have an air of familiarity about it, so Abbie decided not to take offence at his sexist remark . . . since he did have a point about her stopping whilst ahead!

She laughed. 'You can further redeem yourself by helping me to carry some of this lumber inside . . . and then, if you still insist on my moving my car, I'll do my best to oblige, if you'll tell me a good place to park it overnight.'

He seemed taken aback.

'You're staying overnight? Where? Mrs Crompton hasn't moved out of her flat, yet, has she?'

'Grab an armful and you can come and see!' Abbie invited him. 'And I promise not to bite!'

He gave a rueful laugh. 'All right! Since you're winning hands down on this deal, young lady, I may as well give you total victory! Open up the back of your car and let's see what you've got!'

Abbie quickly ran to open the shop door and for the next five minutes they staggered past each other with their arms laden with items.

'That's it! My life laid bare before you!' Abbie said dramatically indicating the spread of her belongings on the floor.

'And now for the tardis!'

'In here!'

Abbie led the way and opened the door into what was now her bed-sit. Considering the amount of her possessions in the other room, it did seem rather small but she was pleased with the room's appearance.

'This is the tidiest you'll see it!' she warned.

He stood in the doorway and glanced around, nodding in reluctant admiration. 'It's unrecognisable from what it was before. You've done a good job with it. Let's hope you do as well with the rest of the place.'

Abbie wasn't sure how sincere that hope was but didn't want to spoil the

delicate truce between them by query-
ing it.

'Right! I'll move my car, then, shall
I?'

'No. It's all right. Leave it where it is.
I'll be leaving again in quarter of an
hour . . . and there should be a space
later.' He grinned again, his face almost
boyish in comparison to his former
glowering expression. 'I'll allow you
'squatter's rights' for now! I'll be off,
then. Goodnight, Miss N . . . ' He
paused. 'Let's not be too formal.' He
held out his hand. 'I'm Tim. Tim
Boardman. And you are?'

'Abigail Norton.'

She took his hand, surprised at how
comfortable and firm his grip was. An
unexpected tingle ran through her body
but she suppressed it immediately.
'Goodnight, Tim. Thanks for your help.'

The next two weeks were extremely
busy and she caught no more than a
few passing glimpses of Tim Boardman.
She had no occasion to step into his
shop and he obviously had no need to

step into hers. That was fine by Abigail. Instinctively distrusting the stability of their declared truce, she wasn't going to go looking for trouble.

Eddie, her carpenter, quickly knocked up the framework for three therapy cubicles and, whilst Abbie donned her decorator's uniform and papered the plywood partitions, Eddie set to and made a nicely-shaped reception desk . . . and an electrician installed the wiring for the piped music and other electrical equipment Abbie would be using.

The plumber grumbled about the old pipe-work in the washroom but the cost of replacing it all was too high for Abigail to contemplate at the moment.

'It's only for three months,' she explained. 'When I'm the owner, I'll get it all done properly.'

The plumber agreed that it wasn't urgent and agreed to obtain a small, compact shower cubicle for her.

The next day, none of the workmen

turned up to work.

Abbie paced back and forth, fuming at their lateness. There was a limit to what she could be doing until their work was finished. She needed them here . . . now! Eventually, at ten thirty, she telephoned first Eddie's number, then the plumber. The office girls at both places gave the same reply.

'But, Miss Norton, you telephoned to cancel today's work. 'Unexpectedly called away', you said; that you'd 'get in touch when work could be resumed'.'

'I certainly did no such thing!' Abbie exclaimed. 'When was this?'

'First thing this morning. It meant a hasty rescheduling of our day's work programme.'

'Well, it wasn't me! What did the person sound like?'

The girl hesitated. 'I'm afraid I can't really say. I didn't take particular notice. I just took the message and rescheduled the work. It didn't occur to me that it wasn't genuine cancellation.'

Abigail chewed her lower lip. Why

should the girl have suspected anything was amiss!

But who would want to cause her any disruption?

Was it just some kids larking about?

A car drew up outside. Tim Boardman's car! He saw her staring at him through the window and waved his hand in a greeting. The half-smile on his face looked more like a satisfied smirk to Abbie . . . and she saw red!

Huh! Look no further!

Who else but Tim Boardman wanted her business to fail?

With no more ado, she flung open her door and stormed outside.

3

'Pleased with yourself, are you?' Abbie greeted Tim angrily, as she halted a few feet in front of him, the backs of her hands placed firmly on her hips.

Tim seemed taken aback but swiftly recovered his composure. His right eyebrow rose questioningly. 'Any reason why I shouldn't be?'

Abbie read sarcasm in his reply. 'No, of course not! You've got what you wanted . . . a delay in the work being done on my property! Well, let me tell you, I'm on to you! And, if it's war you want, then it's war you'll get!

'Whoa! Whoa!' He stepped back, his hands held out in front of him in mock surrender. 'Hold it right there!'

The gesture took her by surprise because she had read an open admission of guilt in his earlier gesture. Now, she felt less sure. 'Someone has cancelled my workmen for today!' she accused.

'And you immediately suspected me?'

'Yes. Well, you do have a motive, don't you? You'd like my business to fail.'

Tim looked exasperated. 'I hope there are no local murders whilst you're around! You'd have me arrested, tried and convicted before I'd had time to defend myself! On second thoughts, miss out the 'tried' bit. You don't seem to believe in 'innocent until proven guilty', do you?'

'Was it you?' Abigail persisted in asking, refusing to back down without a direct answer.

'No, it was not! Does that satisfy you?'

Abbie stared at his face, looking for any sign of guilt, however slight. But she saw none. 'Huh! I suppose it will have to,' she allowed him, ungraciously. 'I'm sorry. You seemed to be rather pleased with yourself. I thought you were gloating.'

Tim shook his head, with a glimmer of a smile tweaking the corners of his lips. 'No. If I were guilty, I'd hide it better than that!' He regarded her mockingly. 'You're quite a firebrand, aren't you? Is that why you've no man in your life? Do you frighten them all away?'

How dare he?

'I've had plenty of men in my life!'

'Had? Like I said, you frighten them away!'

'No, I don't! There's . . . ' She paused.

'Name one!'

She opened and closed her mouth like a fish. She tried not to think of the hurt that her break-up with Jonathan, her previous boyfriend, had caused. She didn't regret it. She'd had no option really, not after she had found out the lies he had told her. How could she ever trust him or any man again? Did they all think a few lies didn't matter?

'What was the man's name? Mark, wasn't it? He's not been around since you moved in,' Tim was saying.

Mark? Her brother? How did he . . . ? Oh, of course, he'd been with her in the estate agent's office when Tim Boardman had made his late arrival.

'Been watching me?' she queried coolly.

'Not particularly . . . one just can't help noticing!'

'Well, not that it's any of your business . . . but Mark is in America for a couple of months. He'll be back!'

'Good!'

Was that a flicker of disappointment in his eyes? Surely not! More likely to be scorn. She eyed him under her lashes. If he weren't so hateful, he'd made a handsome escort.

What was she thinking of! Tim Boardman was the last person she would consider going out with!

'What are you going to do now . . . with your schedule held up? Anything I can do to help? Or would you be afraid I would sabotage everything I touched?' Tim was asking.

'I wouldn't dream of troubling you!'

'Ah, but you do trouble me! Constantly! There must be some point of contact that we can make in peace!'

'I doubt it!' She swung on her heel, adding over her shoulder, 'I'll let you know if I think of anything!'

'You do that! I'll see you around!'

Abigail returned to her salon, musing over the encounter. In spite of their constant misunderstandings, there was something that sparked between them. Maybe, too much of a spark. She didn't want a tempestuous relationship with anyone. She had had enough of that with Jonathan.

Now that Jonathan had intruded into her mind, the unpleasant memories of their break-up lingered there and she recalled how shocked she had been when she had discovered that, unbeknown to her, he was seeing someone else at the same time.

'What's the difference?' he'd asked. 'Fay doesn't know about you . . . and you didn't know about her. You were happy, weren't you? What's all the fuss about?'

'Doesn't trust mean anything to you?'

It hadn't been easy though. They had been seeing each other for nearly six months and now she had nobody. How had he managed to juggle his life for so long without rousing her suspicions? She was too naïve, that was what it was! Mark hadn't been at all surprised when she had tearfully told him.

Thinking of her twin brought a lump to her throat. She was missing him! But he had his own life to lead . . . and she had to get on with hers.

Angry with herself for allowing the memories to intrude into her new life, she brusquely dragged out her laptop and began to design an advertising leaflet to spread throughout the village. She would also put an ad in the local papers for a few weeks. That should bring in some clients.

She was soon engrossed in her work and was surprised to hear the doorbell chime and realise that it was almost one o'clock.

The visitor was Colin Jackson from the estate office in town.

'You've certainly got a move on!' he admired, looking around. 'Are your workmen having a break from it today?'

'No. The 'break' came from other quarters.'

She explained briefly what had happened, omitting her unfounded suspicions about Tim. 'So, I'm doing an advertising leaflet instead, to wile away the time.'

Colin shrugged. 'Well, if you can run some off right now, it's my half-day off this afternoon. I could give you a hand with delivering some.'

Abbie was uncertain. His youthful good looks made him an attractive proposition, but in spite of her stirrings of attraction towards Tim, she truly didn't want any romantic entanglements to get in the way of her new venture.

'No strings attached,' Colin smiled,

as if sensing her imminent rebuff.

Abigail relaxed, chiding herself for her hesitancy. She was missing her circle of casual friends and Colin was pleasant enough . . . even though he didn't set her pulse racing.

'You're on!' she smiled. She wouldn't yet be able to include the date when the salon would open, but that didn't matter. She typed instead, Watch the local press for the opening date. She checked the 'preview' and was satisfied with the chosen format.

'This won't take long,' she said, dragging out the printer. 'Thank goodness I stocked up on paper. I think an initial run of five hundred will be enough. That should keep us busy for the afternoon, shouldn't it? We can always come back and run off some more, if necessary.'

'And, while they're printing, how about a bite of something to eat at The Golden Lion just down the road?' Colin suggested.

Abigail agreed and, after checking the

first few papers through the printer, she locked up the salon and accompanied Colin across the road to the pub next to the church. To her immense satisfaction, Tim was there, having lunch with his snooty receptionist.

Conscious of Colin's hand under her elbow, Abigail beamed at them both.

Tim smiled affably at her, his right eyebrow sardonically raised.

Abbie found the impulse to scowl at him, thinking, I bet he thinks I've telephoned Colin and asked him out to lunch! Well, let him wonder!

The two men merely nodded at each other and Tim's companion made no sign of recognition. Abbie shrugged, unimpressed by her show of bad-manners.

They had a sandwich and shared a basket of chips between them and, once it was eaten, Abbie was eager to begin the leaflet drop. Tim and his receptionist had left before them, so Abbie was spared being under his scrutiny as they returned to the salon for the leaflets.

'Let's start at the Ormskirk end of the village and work our way back, then I can keep a check on where we've been,' Abbie suggested. 'We'll go in your car and park it part way.'

The work on the salon continued the following day and the shower was easily installed. A few days later, the shop front was completely refurbished and a sign-writer was hired to replace the shop with one of her own design.

The remainder of the leaflets were delivered. It took her three days to cover the whole village. Colin helped again on two evenings and, to her surprise, so did Tim.

Colin seemed to feel Tim was intruding on his 'preserve' and made a number of pointed remarks, all of which Tim ignored. In fact, he seemed to find it amusing. Abbie felt caught between them and sided with neither, though the situation threw her emotions into turmoil.

On the final night of delivery, they finished up in The Golden Lion again.

Tim raised his glass. 'To 'Abigail's Aromatherapy Beauty Parlour',' he toasted.

Both men seemed to think it was his duty to escort Abigail back to her salon and she quite enjoyed the sensation, even though she was a bit amused by it. Her amusement ceased when they drew near to the salon. A police car had drawn up in the small parking area and a small group of youths were loitering nearby, sensing the drama about to erupt.

'Oh, no!'

It was Abbie who cried out. She had just seen that the large plate-glass window of her salon had a hole in the centre and thousands of cracks like the rays of the sun bursting out around it!

She darted forward, with Tim at her side and Colin close behind, and drew up in front of the window.

'It's shattered!' she said, stating the obvious . . . but too shocked to be subtle. 'Who'd do a thing like this?'

Tim put an arm around her shoulders, but she shook it off as she whirled round to look at the youths.

'Did any of you see who did it?'

'No, miss!' they chorused.

One of the police officers came over to them. 'Does this property belong to one of you?'

'It's Miss Norton's,' Tim said, indicating her.

'It's mine,' Abigail said at the same time. 'Did anyone see who did it? Who reported it? It must have been done in the past hour. Has the salon been broken into as well?'

'It doesn't look like it,' Colin commented, investigating the door.

'No-one's been inside, miss,' the police officer assured her. 'Now you're here, maybe we can look inside?'

Hundreds of shards of glass lay scattered on the floor. The missile, a lump of stone, had a crudely misspelled message written in unformed script attached to it by a couple of elastic bands. *Go back were you come*

47

from. Your not wonted here!

'Got any idea who might have done it, miss?' one of the officers asked.

Abigail shook her head, although her heart chilled within her. A few days ago, she might have immediately suspected Tim! She wondered if he thought she still might . . . but didn't dare look at him to see what his reaction was.

'No,' she said aloud. 'There have been one or two other incidents, like someone cancelling my workmen . . . but nothing like this.'

Tim's expression didn't alter and Abbie tormented herself by recalling his words, 'If I were guilty, I'd hide it better than that!' She determinedly pushed the recollection away. It had to be someone else! But, who?

'Someone dressed in black was seen running away,' the second officer volunteered, 'but there's no likelihood of him or her being identified. Whoever it was waited until it was dark. We'll give you an incident number for insurance purposes . . . and maybe your friends will see about getting the window boarded up for you. There's nothing more we can do tonight.'

Colin telephoned someone he knew who said he'd be round within the hour to safely board up the window and Tim set to brushing up the glass for her. When the man came to do the boarding up, Tim insisted she and Colin went up to his flat and had a drink of coffee.

It was a subdued end to the evening. When Abbie was ready to go back to her bedsit, Tim insisted on going in with her. She was glad of it. The reaction was setting in and she could feel herself beginning to tremble.

Tim was cheerfully matter-of-fact. 'You'll be all right. You've got your mobile phone handy? Good. Here's my number. If you're worried about anything, give me a call.'

He wrote it down on a scrap of paper and put it on the cupboard then; he helped her pull out the sofa into a bed, and shook out her sleeping bag. Just before he went, he held her briefly, murmuring, 'Sleep tight!'

His lips briefly touched her forehead, sending a frisson of pleasure spiralling through her, but he didn't seem to notice.

The broken window was replaced with toughened glass two days later; the indoor décor completed a few days after that; and all the necessary equipment bought and installed with no further delay.

For the first few days, Abbie found herself feeling anxious whilst away from the salon and apprehensive on her return until she could see that all was well . . . but her tension eased as each day passed with no further incident.

With everything in place, or almost so, she prepared a large banner to hang in the window proclaiming that the salon was to open the following Tuesday. The first two days' treatments were to be on special offer at half-price with a selection of free short-treatments to be demonstrated on willing volunteers at the Grand Opening Ceremony throughout the Monday.

All local businesses were issued private invitations and among her first 'guinea pigs' at the Opening Ceremony were the 'flower girls', as she privately thought of them . . . who enjoyed a facial, manicure and foot massage between them. Tim volunteered for an Indian Head Massage, to the amusement of many on-lookers. His receptionist, now introduced as Corinda Jones, politely declined to participate.

'She's perfect enough already!' Liz, one of the flower girls, whispered in Abbie's ear.

With a selection of wine available throughout the day, the occasion was a huge success and Abigail enjoyed a surge of excitement when she locked up for the night. She was *up and running*, highly optimistic for the future and full of boundless energy — she could face anything!

4

Which was just as well, since the appointments began to trickle in . . . hands to be manicured, eyelashes to be curled and eyebrows shaped, facials, leg-waxings, pedicures and full-body massages . . . and by the time her first week ended, Abbie's appointment book was looking quite well-filled for the following week. If business remained as brisk as this, she would soon need to think about employing an assistant.

Then the bills began to roll in. Astronomical bills, with amounts so high that they took Abigail's breath away. No way had she used that amount of electricity! And why a water bill so soon? The glazier's bill would have serviced the whole row of business premises! The sign-writer had only quoted a quarter of the declared amount.

Abigail began to phone the various utility services involved and incurred a number of confusing conversations, all of which came, eventually, to the same conclusion. The bills were false, albeit very cleverly done using a photocopier and computer. The phantom trickster had struck again.

The most worrying aspect was that, whoever the culprit was, he or she must be sited in the close vicinity, as all the bogus billheads were reputedly from the tradesmen she had used. Abigail gathered all the phoney bills together and took them next door to show to Tim.

He shook his head over them. 'Someone has got it in for you, Abbie. You don't still think it's me, do you?'

'No, of course not!' she said just a shade too quickly . . . since a niggling doubt of his innocence persisted in plaguing her peace of mind. Who else would want to destroy her business venture?

Sure, there was another beauty salon

at the other end of the village . . . but it was a long village and boasted of more than one of many businesses. There were countless hairdressers; two news-agents, chemists, small supermarkets, doctors' surgeries, dentists and others. All thrived side-by-side.

Thankful to bid farewell to her final customer of her second week, Abbie nipped across the road to the supper bar that was situated opposite to her and bought her favourite Chinese food — Chop Suey Special with fried rice; made herself a cool drink; and pressed the remote control switch of her portable television. A bit of Saturday night viewing would give her aching muscles a rest.

Maybe she shouldn't have refused Colin's invitation to the cinema? He was pushing forward far too quickly for her peace of mind. In the back of her mind, she felt uncomfortable about him, as she knew she saw him only as a friend, whereas he seemed to hope for something more. Still, she had told him how she felt, so it was up to him if he continued to see her.

She yawned widely. Bed called!

She wasn't sure how long she had been asleep when she was suddenly awakened by something. She lay completely still. What had woken her?

A noise above drew her eyes up towards the ceiling. There it was again. It sounded like something being dragged across the floor and then dumped heavily. Whatever it was . . . someone was up there. Someone who had no right to be there. Was it the same person who had thrown the brick through her window? Her heart thumped alarmingly.

What should she do? She had no way of getting into the flat . . . and, even if she had, it could be dangerous to tackle the intruder on her own.

She remained still, listening for more sounds . . . but none came. Had she imagined the noises? Or, were they from the two properties on either side of her? She knew that no-one lived above the flower shop . . . but Tim lived in the flat over his travel firm. Maybe he had been doing some late-night furniture moving?

She remained alert for ages, deciding that if she heard one more sound, she would immediately ring Tim . . . if she could find his number . . . but she heard nothing else and she eventually fell asleep again, convinced that she had imagined or dreamed the sounds.

She awoke the following morning to the sound of the church bells ringing and lay for a few minutes enjoying the melodious sound, realising that she would be too late to attend the morning service herself. She yawned, surprised at the lateness of the hour and then remembered her broken sleep.

She decided that, for her peace of mind, she would have to ask Tim if he had been up late, maybe moving things in the room next to the one over her bedsit.

It was a bright early autumn day, so she showered; dressed in a light trouser suit; ate a hasty breakfast; and then went outside to the shop next door and rang the bell to the upstairs flat.

Tim's voice sounded at her ear-level. 'Hello! Who is it?'

'Oh! It's me, Abigail.'

'Are you all right?' he asked sharply.

'Yes. I just need to see you for a minute.'

'Right. Push the door when you hear the buzz and come up,' he invited.

Abigail did as requested and pushed open the outer door. The door at the top opened when she was nearly at the top of the stairs and Tim appeared, dressed in a terry bathrobe. He yawned widely but smothered it with a hand.

'Good morning, Abigail! To what do I owe the pleasure of your visit? Oh, excuse me!' as he yawned again. 'I had a late night last night, I'm afraid and I'm not quite awake yet!'

'Oh, so it was you!' Abigail said in relief as she reached the landing.

'What was me?' Tim demanded. 'What am I guilty of now?'

Abigail laughed, stepping past him into his living room. 'Nothing bad this time. Only I'm sure I heard some noises in the night. They seemed to come from the flat above me . . . but no-one should be up there, should they? I decided that it was probably you up to something or other . . . and I was right. That's a relief!'

'Except that I wasn't!'

'Wasn't what?'

'Up to anything . . . anything other than sleeping, that is. I got in at about two in the morning and went straight to bed. Whatever you heard, it wasn't caused by me!'

That threw her theory out of the window. 'Are you sure?'

'Of course I'm sure! And, no, I don't walk in my sleep and no, I don't believe in poltergeists either! Now, are you sure you heard noises?'

'I think so. It seemed real at the time. Footsteps, someone moving something. Then it stopped and I wasn't sure. It seemed to come from right above me.

Has anyone got a key?'

Tim looked amused. 'Your friend, Colin Jackson, has one. You don't suppose he has secretly moved in above you? No? Well, apart from Mrs Crompton herself, as far as I know, I'm the only other person with a key.'

'You? Why have you got a key?'

'Because, unlike you, Mrs Crompton trusts me implicitly!'

Abigail had the grace to blush. 'Sorry!' she murmured. 'I probably don't know you as well as she does.'

Tim grinned, enjoying her discomfort. 'Give me a few minutes to get dressed and we'll go and see what it's like up there.'

Abigail sat on the edge of his sofa and leafed through a magazine while she waited. True to his word, he took only a few minutes to dress and, though unshaven, was ready to accompany her to the flat.

It was very similar to Tim's flat and she knew she could be happy here. She looked around with interest, thinking ahead to the time when it would be hers.

There was a spacious living room, decorated in a pale cream. Mrs Crompton's furniture was old, but had been looked after and went well with the room. A number of large boxes were stacked to one side; some fastened down with tape, others partly open.

'I've been helping Mrs Crompton start her packing,' Tim explained, seeing where her glance had fallen.

Abigail nodded. He was a good neighbour to the old lady . . . maybe, eventually, a good neighbour to her?

He pursed his lips thoughtfully. 'Someone might have been up here, but who? As far as I know, her only relative is a n'er-do-well nephew . . . and I'm sure she wouldn't have given him a key to her flat. She hasn't a good word to say about him.'

He stepped back into the living room and glanced about. 'The sofa might have been moved. I'm sure it was nearer the window.' He spread his hands uncertainly. 'All I can suggest is that I ask her next time I visit ... without trying to worry her, of course. And I suggest that you keep your ears open and, if you hear any more noises up here, give me a buzz and I'll come round and look. I'll give you one of my business cards when we go down.'

'It was in the middle of the night! I can't disturb you then!'

'That's all right. I'd rather get it solved. There's no sign of a break-in, so, if someone is getting in, I'm sure Mrs Crompton would like to know about it. Anyway, there's nothing else we can do up here. Like it, do you?'

Abigail nodded. 'Yes, it's very nice. It will be great to move in, especially after the cramped quarters downstairs.'

Yes, she'd do very nicely up here ... once it was hers!

Back outside, they paused outside the door to Abbie's Salon. 'Er, thanks for going up to check the place,' Abbie said hesitantly, somehow reluctant to simply go back into her bedsit.

The day was too lovely to be indoors, especially on her own. But, what alternative was there? A run out in her car?

As if of the same mind, Tim looked at her quizzically. 'Well, Miss Prickly Pear, dare I ask you to come out for lunch with me? Somewhere like Southport or for a walk along the canal bank at Parbold?'

Abbie felt her breath catch in her throat. Go out for lunch with him?

'Why do you call me that?' she asked, evading his question until her heart settled down again.

He laughed. 'Because you bristle with prickles every time you come near me! Is this a relic from some past boy-friend? Someone who treated you, shall we say, unkindly? Mark, perhaps?'

'Oh, not Mark!'

'Someone else, then? Someone before Mark? Someone who betrayed your trust?'

How right he was! She hadn't been

aware that Jonathan's betrayal had made so obvious a mark on her.

'Perhaps,' she said, as nonchalantly as she could . . . then, to steer away from touchy ground, she asked, 'Out to lunch, did you say? It sounds good to me.'

'Great! Give me half-an-hour to make myself presentable . . . and I'll be all yours for the day!'

Abbie felt herself unaccountably filled with nervous excitement as she wiled away the half-hour tidying away her breakfast dishes.

She felt on edge as she slid into the front passenger seat beside Tim and busily set about fastening her seat belt as they set off to hide her agitation. Tim pressed the button that slid back the sunroof and the warm autumn breeze ruffled through her hair, bringing a sense of peace to her.

Tim passed comment on the various places they passed through and, by the time they were passing through the market town of Ormskirk, Abigail found herself relaxed and responding naturally.

By the time they arrived at Southport and parked at the southern end of the Marine Drive facing the sea, they were laughing together like old friends and Abigail wondered why she had felt so antagonistic to him at first.

The sun was warm, so she left her light cardigan in the car and, hand-in-hand, they strolled along the sea front a little way and then turned towards the town and had a delicious lunch in The Prince Of Wales Hotel. Afterwards, they strolled along Lord Street, a wide tree-lined boulevard with shops and hotels on both sides that spoke of the town's former opulent years a century earlier.

A pleasant park was at the northern end of the town and they sat on the grass, hands clasped around their knees, sharing events from their childhood that had them both laughing and remarking on the many similarities of their formative years. And, of course,

Abbie admitted that Mark was her twin brother.

'And there's no-one else?' Tim asked softly, tucking a wisp of hair behind her ear.

'Not at the moment,' Abigail replied. 'Good! I'm glad about that!'

He lay back on the grass and clasped his hands behind his head, a satisfied smile just lifting the corners of his mouth. Abigail stayed as she was for a while, resting her chin on her knees as she stared unseeingly ahead, wondering if she had shared too much about herself. Hadn't she vowed not to trust anyone so readily again?

When she glanced down at Tim, his eyes were closed and she was sure he had fallen asleep. Well, he had said he was up late the previous night, hadn't he? She lay down beside him, propping up her head on her left hand, her elbow on the ground and gazed down at his face.

His dark eyelashes fanned out over his cheeks and she let her eyes trace the line of his cheekbones down to his firm chin, where there was a teeny-tiny nick of dried blood that showed he had cut himself shaving that morning. Had he felt as nervous as she had? She smiled at the thought.

A small twitch at the side of his wonderful sensual mouth made her wonder if he were awake but his eyes didn't open, so she decided he was dreaming about something nice. Was it her?

The thought gave her a longing to kiss him and, holding her breath lest she disturbed him, she lowered her head and gently fluttered her lips against his.

When his hand suddenly clasped her head to his, she almost screamed in fright but found it was impossible to lift herself away from him . . . and the kiss was so delicious that she relaxed into it and enjoyed it immensely.

'You were pretending to be asleep!' she accused him when they paused to take breath.

On the way home, he drove through the country lanes to avoid the traffic and they stopped and had dinner at The Saracen's Head by the canal, which they strolled along for a while afterwards, until the sun went down and Abigail needed her cardigan.

'It's been a wonderful day!' she thanked him on her doorstep.

He dropped a kiss onto the top of her head, thanked her for sharing a lovely day with him and, after seeing her safely inside her salon, bade her, 'Goodnight . . . and pleasant dreams!'

No! She couldn't let this happen! Jonathan's betrayal of her still hurt too much to allow her to risk another heartbreak.

She didn't want uncertainties. Her new business was taking off so well and she needed to be free to develop it further. Romance was something she could definitely do without right now!

★　★　★

It was after eight o'clock when Abbie awoke the next day.

She sank back against her pillow, memories of a certain handsome face flooding back with a vengeance.

How would they react when they met? Was Tim having regrets as well?

A glance at the clock made her leap out of bed, shower and dress more quickly than usual and then haul her sleeping bag off the sofa-bed and transform it into a sofa once more.

After swallowing a hasty breakfast of muesli and fresh orange juice she rushed into the front reception area to take a detailed look at her diary. The first appointment was at nine o'clock — *eyebrows and make-up.*

That was followed by a full facial at half-past nine and a full aromatherapy massage at half-past ten.

She was partway through the manicure when the doorbell pinged as someone entered the reception area.

'Excuse me a moment,' she apologised to her client. 'I won't be a minute.'

The sooner she could afford to employ someone on reception, the better, she reflected as she placed the brush back into the bottle of nail varnish and screwed back the lid, before going to see who had come in.

'Oh!'

The immaculately-groomed woman idly leafing through a magazine on the counter was Corinda Jones, Tim's receptionist.

Abbie bit back the words, 'What do you want?' saying instead, 'Good morning! How can I help you today?'

Corinda held out her slender hand, indicating a ragged nail on her index finger.

'As you see, my nail is ruined!' she pouted. 'Tim insists that I have it fixed right away! He does like the women around him to be elegant at all times, you know.'

'Really?' Abbie murmured coolly, thinking how windblown she must have looked yesterday. She pulled forward her appointments book. 'I'll write you in at twenty-past, Miss Jones. If you will take a seat, I'll be with you as soon as I am able.'

Abbie returned to her client, feeling slightly disadvantaged by Corinda's impeccable style. Was that really how Tim preferred his women? It must take her hours to get herself to look like that every morning!

She gave a rueful laugh as she seated herself at the manicure table, recognising her own 'sour grapes'. What did she care? Hadn't she already decided to cool it with Tim?

When she eventually invited Corinda to follow her through to the manicure table, Abigail was totally professional, making a little casual conversation as was usually expected.

'Not bad,' Corinda commented. 'I don't suppose anyone will notice it, anyhow.' Her red lips smiled, though Abigail noticed that the smile didn't reach her eyes. They held a cool, calculating gleam.

'Did I mention that Tim is taking me

out to dinner tonight? A full-evening dress affair in Manchester. It's so important to make a good impression at these affairs, isn't it? Having the right sort of partner and so on? All our friends comment on what an ideal couple we make!'

Abigail felt her heart sink.

Even though she had resolved not to take the budding relationship any further, she was disappointed to realise that he hadn't told her that he was already involved with Corinda.

'Is that so?' she said through tight lips.

Corinda laid her perfectly-restored fingertips on Abigail's arm. 'Don't take it too badly, dear,' she murmured in patronising tones. 'Tim told me all about your little outing yesterday. We don't have secrets, you see. We have what we call an 'open' relationship.

Abigail's throat felt too tight to reply. She felt totally humiliated. How could he lead her on like that?

But, oh, it hurt to discover that Tim was no different from Jonathan.

5

Abigail couldn't wait for lunchtime to arrive. She made herself a hasty sandwich which she ate in her bedsit, determined not to let the threatening tears to flow. She had vowed that no man would make her cry again!

At one o'clock she was ready and waiting for her first appointment to arrive.

She waited in vain. The woman didn't turn up.

The third and fourth appointments were kept, with two more missed by closing time. She was sure she'd written them in the right place, though it sometimes got a bit hectic when she was in the midst of a treatment and a prospective client either popped in or telephoned to make an appointment.

Abigail knew a certain percentage of appointments were missed in businesses such as hers . . . people forgot or something else cropped up . . . but it was disappointing, all the same, especially three in one day! What she needed was a trainee to man the desk.

She had just wished goodbye to her final client of the day when the phone rang. Swiftly locking her door, she went over to the phone, pen poised to book in another client.

'Hello? Abigail's Aromatherapy Beauty Parlour. Abigail speaking. May I help you?'

'Abbie!' a voice squealed in her ear. 'It's me! Jenny! You do sound posh! How are you, kid? I thought I'd just look you up to see how you're getting on. What's it like, being your own boss? Great, eh?'

'Hi, Jenny. It's good to hear from you. You've been out the last few times I've called. Got a new boyfriend, eh?'

'Er . . . yes and no.' Jenny's voice hesitantly dismissed the topic. 'But, what about you? How are you doing?'

They had been friends since they had

met at the college on the 'Aroma-therapy And Massage' course and had worked together in Abbie's previous job, though things hadn't seemed to be going too well between them in the few weeks before she left. She grimaced. That was probably due to her own preoccupation with her relationship with Jonathan going sour. No wonder Jenny had kept her distance from her.

At the end, Jenny had even seemed relieved that Abbie was moving on.

It had been the right decision, Abbie was still sure.

This was a great opportunity for her to branch out on her own . . . or it had been . . . until today!

'I'm doing fine!' Abigail hastily exclaimed, forcing a brightness into her voice that she was far from feeling. 'Plenty of bookings! I'm beginning to wonder if I could do with a part-time assistant.'

'Great! I . . . er . . . might be able to help you there, Abbie.'

'Oh? Do you know someone suitable

who needs a job?'

Jenny laughed. 'Myself!'

Abigail was stunned. 'You? But, you've got a job! You haven't jacked it in, have you?' knowing her friend's volatile disposition.

'N . . . no . . . but I'm thinking of it. I've told Miss Speight that I'm taking a week or two's holiday. I'm due some leave anyway.'

'Fine! Well, if you're sure, I could do with a bit of help, even if only for a week or so to see how things go.'

Abigail suddenly remembered her limited living quarters. 'Mind you, I was thinking more of someone local. I'm a bit squashed for space until the upstairs flat becomes available. I've only got a sofa bed for us to sleep on. Will it do for a night or two until you decide what you're doing?'

'Yes. We can sleep top-to-toe. We've done that plenty of times.'

'So we have. Bring your own sleeping bag and a pillow. It'll be great seeing you again, Jenny. When can you come?'

'How about this evening?'

'Great! Will you be driving?'

'Yes.'

Abigail gave her the details of how to find her and they ended the conversation full of promises of good times together.

'Gosh, Abbie! This is lovely!' Jenny enthused as Abigail opened the door and let her in. 'You've done wonders already. Lucky you! Things always did go well for you. I reckon you were born under a lucky star?'

'There's no such thing,' Abbie reminded her, remembering it had been Jenny's constant gripe. 'Hard work and sticking at it is what gets you places! Anyway, fetch your things through and I'll show you our living arrangements. You're sure you'll be all right on the sofa with me?'

'Sure thing, babe! It's better than camping!'

Abigail laughed. 'Whenever did you try camping? I wouldn't have thought it was your style!'

'Too right! That's what I mean. Anything is better than that! And getting Miss High and Mighty Speight out of my hair!'

Abigail was bemused. 'I take it you don't get on with her any better than you did!'

'Not so you'd notice!' Jenny shrugged. 'She's only one rung higher than me as you know . . . but boy, does she revel in it! At least I'll be level-pegging here with you!'

'Except, I am the boss!' Abigail spoke lightly, but she saw a frown flicker across Jenny's face. 'Will coffee be all right?'

'Thanks.' Jenny flopped down on to the sofa. She looked up at Abigail, her face unusually serious. 'I'm really looking forward to this, you know. You've no idea what it means to me.'

'Is there something you're not telling me, Jenny?'

'No! No, of course not!' Jenny looked flustered for a moment. 'It's just great to be together again, isn't it? What sort of treatments are you offering? All the usual ones? What have you got lined up for me to do?'

Abigail looked at her suspiciously, but Jenny's face reflected only eager curiosity. 'If you nip back into the reception area, you'll see the appointments diary on the desk. Be a love and fetch it in. We can go through it as soon as we've eaten. I've ordered a take-away from across the road. Is that okay?'

It was . . . and they chatted happily as they ate it, catching up on each other's current state of life. Abigail was reluctant to talk about Tim, though.

Was she afraid that Jenny would read too much into it? Or that she would make it her business to wheedle out of her every last detail of every sentence they had said to each other? But it was still too recent and painful for that.

Surprisingly, Jenny was sparse on details of her own recent love-life. 'There's no-one at the moment, kid. You know how it is. Men come and go. I've had enough of them for the time being. Er . . . how do you feel about Jonathan? Still reeling from the shock, eh?'

Abigail bristled 'No! I've wiped him clean off my memory! I might have well asked, 'Jonathan who?''

'Are you sure?'

'Perfectly! Why? Have you heard anything I ought to know?'

'N . . . no. I just wanted to make sure you were over him. You're probably better off without him, aren't you?'

'I think so! I just felt such a fool. How could I not know that he was two-timing me? That he already had another girlfriend? I must have been blind! And how must Fay have felt? She probably blames me for stealing her man!'

'It happens all the time, kid. Sometimes, people just can't help themselves. You know, they meet eyes across a crowded room and wham! They're in love! They don't think about the other person.'

Abigail felt shocked. 'Is that what you

think about me? That I just didn't care about Fay?'

'No! I was meaning Jonathan. That's what he's like . . . unfortunately. He only sees what is happening to him. I don't think he's aware about what's happening to the person he's betraying.'

Abigail looked at her sharply. She sounded . . . sad. She reached across and touched Jenny's hand. 'It's all right, Jenny. It's sweet of you to care, but I'm completely over him, honestly.' She smiled . . . and was glad to see Jenny smile in return.

'It's all water under the bridge. I've got a new life here. New business, new home, new start.'

'And new man?'

Abigail shook her head. 'Not yet. I'm not even looking! One thing at once, I say.'

'Good! I'll drink to that!' Jenny lifted her glass of wine. 'A new start . . . for both of us!'

At half-past ten the following day,

Abigail wondered why she had bothered to be so reticent. She was part-way through a manicure when she had heard the bell ring, announcing the arrival of someone into reception.

Jenny was taking payment from her latest client. Abigail heard her voice as she welcomed whoever it was. Wow, from the tone of her voice it must be some client!

She glanced up . . . and her heart somersaulted.

It was Tim Boardman. He had a cheek!

She felt her face freeze. She didn't want to speak to him! Not here! Not ever!

Tim had other ideas.

'Hi!' He beamed at the two ladies waiting in reception, including Jenny, in his sweeping glance. He stepped towards Abigail, seemingly taking no offence when she didn't rise from her seat.

'Sorry! I can see it's not a convenient time, Abbie!' he apologised as he strode nearer. 'I just wanted to say I'm sorry I couldn't get in to see you yesterday. Did Corinda give you my message?'

Abbie looked at him coldly.

'She did.'

Tim looked taken aback by the lack of warmth in her voice. It halted him in his tracks.

'Right! Er . . . it was just one of those things and couldn't be helped. You know how it is!'

'Only too well! Was there anything else you wanted?'

'Well, er, not right now, it seems.'

Abigail felt she could have laughed if she hadn't been so hurt by his nonchalant carousing. He looked totally at a loss what to say. Expected her to fall at his feet and continue as though nothing untoward had happened, did he?

After a moment's hesitation, he recovered his poise. He straightened his tie, as if smoothing out its wrinkles would sort out the hiccups in his life, and smiled around with great charm.

'Excuse me for intruding, ladies. Obviously a bad moment!'

He brought his gaze back to settle on Abigail, who had resumed her work on her client's nails. The tone of his voice altered as he said, 'I'll see you later, Abbie. Shall we say six o'clock?'

He lifted his hand in salute and turned on his heels. With another wave from the door, he was gone, making the salon seem empty by his departure.

'Well!' Jenny whistled. 'You certainly kept quiet about him!'

'I'm not surprised!' her client murmured appreciatively. 'I'd keep pretty quiet myself about a hunk like that!'

'I hardly know him,' Abigail protested, aware that her cheeks were burning.

'What do you need to know?' Jenny laughed. 'No wonder you moved down here, if that's what the local menfolk are like!'

'He's all right,' Abigail shrugged, resuming the application of nail polish.

Jenny pulled a face. 'He's more than

all right! He's an absolute 'Wow!' in my opinion!' She paused and eyed Abigail's determined show of indifference. 'Well, if you're not interested, I certainly am!' she added as she returned to reception where another client was waiting.

Abigail watched her go with dismay. Had she protested too much? Because, deep down in her heart, she knew she was still interested in him! But was she ready to face the uncertainties of early courtship?

Especially in the face of a rival? Two rivals with Jenny now on the scene!

The salon closed at half-past five and, with careful nonchalance, Abigail showered, changed into a neat pair of casual trousers, brushed her hair until it gleamed and applied a little make-up.

On the stroke of six, the doorbell pinged and Tim entered the salon . . . where Abigail just happened to be sorting through the array of magazines she kept handy for her clients to browse through whilst waiting for their appointment.

Tim looked at her with exaggerated wariness. 'Is it safe for me to come in?' he asked. 'You're not going to throw that magazine at me, are you?'

Abigail glanced down at the article in her hands.

'Certainly not!' she said crisply. 'I don't throw things!'

'Would you care to take a walk with me? There's a lovely stroll across the fields behind the church . . . a rustic bridge across a tiny stream.'

The unbidden memory of lying on the grass in the park surge into Abbie's inner vision . . . quickly followed by what had happened next!

'Whatever you have to say can be said right here!' she snapped.

'Ok, that's fine by me.'

He stepped forward and Abigail swiftly slipped behind the desk, distrusting her body's reaction if Tim were to take hold of her . . . try to kiss her. The evasive action didn't go unnoticed.

Tim rested his hands on the desk and watched her thoughtfully. 'Why so wary of me, Abigail? What's happened since Sunday afternoon? I thought we were . . . getting along just fine.'

'Huh!'

'Did I go too quickly for you? Is that it? I know you've been hurt in the past but not all men are the same.' His voice softened. 'I won't hurt you, Abbie . . . not intentionally.'

He sounded sincere. Abbie briefly chewed her lower lip. 'The fact is, Tim, I don't go in for 'shared relationships',' she said frankly. 'OK, there are casual friendships . . . and that's fine — as long as all parties agree . . . but, anything closer and . . . well, I . . . '

She broke off in embarrassment. Good heavens, she was jumping the gun, wasn't she? They had only had one date! It was just that it had held so much promise . . . and then Corinda had revealed her involvement . . . and she just couldn't bear to get entangled in a threesome again!

'Did Corinda tell you I was taking her to the dinner yesterday evening? Is

that it?' Tim asked, a light of understanding dawning in his eyes.

'Yes.'

And a lot more, she might have
added.

'It was purely a business arrangement,' Tim hastened to explain. 'It was
arranged weeks ago . . . before I'd even
met you. It was an annual Travels
Agents Promotion Evening. You know
the sort of thing.'

'You didn't mention it!'

'I didn't think about it! I had other
things on my mind!'

'Such as?'

He reached over the desk and took
hold of her hand.

Abigail blushed.

'I haven't been a recluse, Abbie. I've
taken out plenty of women over the
years . . . but never more than one at a
time. Don't you believe me?'

'Corinda said that you have an 'open'
relationship with each other. I thought
she meant . . . '

He raised an eyebrow. 'That I take

her out regularly? It's not so. Like I said, I've taken her out on a number of occasions ... but generally in the pursuance of business. She knows the trade. She makes a good business partner ... but nothing more!'

The pads of his thumbs were gently stroking the backs of her hands. He drew her forward gently and leaned over the desk to brush his lips against hers.

A tremor ran through her, as her body responded ... just as she'd known it would.

'Is everything all right?' Jenny's voice suddenly cut in. 'Oh, sorry! Everything was so quiet, I thought you must have gone.'

The last remark was directed straight at Tim and her admiring gaze quite frankly ran over him from head to toe.

Tim seemed to be amused, as if he were quite used to such a reaction from women.

He smiled and nodded towards

Jenny. 'Hi! I didn't realise anyone else was here.'

'Obviously not!' Jenny grinned. 'I'm the new live-in assistant!'

'Right! I saw you earlier, didn't I?' Tim remembered.

Abbie reckoned she had better introduce them. 'Meet Jenny, a long-time friend of mine. She's come to help me out for this week. Jenny, this is Tim Boardman. He owns the travel firm next door.'

Jenny glided forward, her face radiant. She held out her hand to grasp Tim's, but also lifted up her cheek, obviously expecting a more personal greeting.

Tim turned back to Abigail. 'I was hoping you would like to come out to dinner tonight.'

Abigail's heart missed a beat. She swallowed hard as her insides did a double flip. What was it she had decided earlier? Wasn't it not to take it any further! Not to get involved?

Tim smiled, the crinkle lines around

his eyes etched deeply. 'The invitation includes Jenny, of course. Shall we say eight o'clock?'

The refusal on Abigail's lips was swept away by Jenny's swift acceptance. 'That will be lovely, Tim. We'll look forward to that. Won't we, Abbie?'

'Er . . . yes. Thanks,' she added weakly.

Tim moved towards the door. 'Good! I'll see you later, then, ladies.'

6

It wasn't a successful evening . . . not as far as Abigail was concerned. Tim picked them up at the promised time and took them to The Wiggin Tree at the top of Parbold Hill, overlooking the wide expanse of the west Lancashire Plain. It was a pub with a difference, where the many of the tables were around a small dance floor.

Jenny had dressed to kill with a scarlet low-necklined dress that showed off her tan from an early holiday in Spain. The skirt, pinching in a narrow waist, swirled seductively around her legs. Resentment flowed over Abigail as Jenny, true to her earlier promise of making a play for Tim, leaned forward across the table showing off her figure.

Abigail didn't know what was the matter with her. Maybe it was lingering memory of what Corinda had said the previous morning that made her laughter sound false and brittle as she responded to Jenny and Tim's lively chatter. She toyed with her food . . . succulent Dublin Bay prawns for starters and grilled lemon sole for main course . . . and sipped at the wine.

Tim was charming. He shared his attention between his two guests with an ease that spoke of much practice, asking questions about their families and their friendship together. Jenny seemed able to make the dullest occasions sound interesting and she wittily responded to Tim's light-hearted conversation.

Abigail felt herself sinking lower and lower. She wasn't usually like this. She knew it was mainly the reaction to her fear of Tim turning out like Jonathan that had somehow robbed her of her self-confidence, made all the worse by Jenny's animated behaviour.

The desserts, the restaurant's main specialities, were 'out of this world' and when Jenny laughingly told Tim that

Abbie's major vice was a fondness for chocolate, she succumbed to the promise of *Death by Chocolate* in an valiant attempt to join in the light-heartedness of her two companions.

Jenny declined a dessert, declaring that she felt 'too full for words' and asked for a black coffee, instead. Just after the waiter had served the coffee, a quartet began to play dance music.

'Oh, goodie!' Jenny exclaimed in delight. 'I love dancing!' She touched Tim's arm. 'Do you dance, Tim?'

He smiled. 'Yes, I do . . . but . . . '

'Oh, Abbie won't mind if we leave her to finish her chocolate dream! She knows how much I love dancing!' She turned to Abigail, her eyes alight with eagerness. 'You don't mind, do you, Abbie? Please say if you'd rather we didn't!'

Abigail did mind! Very much so! But she smiled brightly, hoping her true feelings didn't show. 'Of course, go ahead. Don't mind me.'

Tim looked unconvinced but laughed

as Jenny pulled him to his feet. 'All right! All right! If you insist! We won't be long,' he said to Abigail as he was dragged towards the dance floor.

They danced so well together. Tim was an as accomplished dancer as Jenny and they effortlessly 'quick-stepped' around the small area, drawing many glances of admiration.

Jenny's dark hair was almost the same shade as Tim's and, as he bent his head to listen to something Jenny was saying to him. Abbie couldn't tell where one head ended and the other began. She sighed, wishing it were her being held so lightly in his arms.

She danced with him later, but felt heavy and dowdy in comparison to Jenny's lightness of step, convinced that Tim would rather be dancing each dance with Jenny instead of only alternately.

How she wished they were on their own. It might have been as magical as Sunday afternoon in the park!

She was glad when they decided to

leave and did her best to respond to Tim's conversation on the way home. She half-heartedly invited him in for coffee and was glad when he declined. All she wanted was to get to bed and see an end to the day.

Jenny had other ideas! 'Oh, what a wonderful evening! I feel like I've been to heaven and back!' her voice trilled in ecstasy as she twirled around. 'Tim and I dance together so well, don't we? I really enjoyed myself! I think Tim did so, too. You didn't mind Tim dancing with me so much, did you, Abbie? I told him you wouldn't mind . . . that you'd said you weren't interested in him as a boyfriend or anything like that. You did say that, didn't you?'

Despair hit Abigail. Jenny was right. She had said that . . . but she hadn't meant it! She mumbled something inaudible and turned her face into the pillow, longing for Jenny to switch off the light. She was interested in Tim. Very much so . . . but was it now too late to admit it . . . either to Jenny or to Tim?

The following day, Abigail awakened with the determination not to let Jenny sideline her where Tim was concerned. Jenny had only monopolised him for one evening, for heaven's sake! It didn't mean she owned him!

Jenny had always been a man-chaser — with no conscience! Only she had never chased Abbie's boyfriends before. So much for thinking their friendship had been the deterrent!

Soon after Abbie had slid back the bolts on the front door and was standing by the desk looking to see what treatment the first client had booked, a movement at the door caught her eye and she saw a slim figure dressed in black leather motorcycling gear leaving the open porch she shared with the upstairs flat.

Before she had caught more than a glimpse, the figure had gone.

Abbie's eyes widened. Was this the mysterious intruder who had disturbed her sleep a few nights ago? She raced to the door, pausing only to pick up an envelope on the floor beneath the letter-box. She caught her breath. It had been hand-delivered and was addressed, *To whoom it mite consern*.

The badly-formed letters were suspiciously like the ones wrapped around the brick that had smashed her window. Is that what the black-leather-clad figure had been doing? Delivering another warning or threat?

She pulled open the door and ran outside, looking left and right . . . but there was no sign of the person. She ran past the flower shop to the next street and was just in time to see such a motorcyclist kick-start a motorbike halfway up the street.

'Hey! Excuse me!' she called out . . . but the motorcyclist either didn't hear or chose to ignore her . . . and zoomed away.

Abbie returned to the salon, the envelope in her hand, looking at it thoughtfully. She felt reluctant to open it, not wanting to read evidence of someone's hate against her, but knew it had to be faced. She slit it open and smoothed out the paper.

The words were, *I no egsackly wot you are doing evry minit of the day!*

It wasn't much of a threat in itself . . . but, seen as part of the recent 'hate campaign', it made Abigail feel uneasy.

It implied someone was closely watching her — as she had already worked out for herself. She glanced through the window, a shiver running down her spine. The rows of shops opposite . . . the Chinese Take-Away, a charity shop, a hairdresser's and a cake shop . . . looked innocent enough. Did they have flats over them, as on her side of the road? She would make it her business to find out.

'What's that you've got?' Jenny asked, coming into the reception area.

Abigail showed it to her, explaining what had just happened.

Jenny pursed her lips. 'Looking at the writing, it could just be kids.'

Abigail felt doubtful. 'Anyone can deliberately mis-spell a few words and scrawl an untidy message. The phoney bills, for example, were too cleverly done to be kids.'

'So, what are you going to do? Contact the police? They've got the other message on file, haven't they?'

'Yes. I'll do that. I'll nip along to the police station in our lunch hour.'

And, she would mention it to Tim and ask him to check the upstairs flat again, just in case the person had been up there. Was someone using the flat and didn't want her down below maybe hearing sounds of occupation?

Feeling more like her usual self, she flung herself into the series of treatments that were booked for that day.

She assigned Jenny to do a full-body massage for a new client, whilst she, in the next cubicle, dealt with another client who was part-way through a course of muscle-toning treatment that was gaining in popularity.

When all of that was progressing

nicely, she plucked the eyebrows of another client and gave her a facial treatment, taking great satisfaction in enabling her clients to look their best and, in some cases, restoring their confidence in themselves.

'See you on Friday, Anne,' she eventually bade farewell to her client. 'It will be the last session. You'll look great on holiday!'

The phone trilled and Abigail picked it up. 'Hello? Abigail's Aromatherapy Beauty Parlour. Abigail speaking. May I help you?'

'Abbie!'

Her heart began to beat quickly.

'Tim! Nice to hear from you! How are you?'

'Fine, thank you.'

His tone softened as he continued, 'Look, Abbie, I'm sorry the evening didn't go quite as I planned. Jenny's very nice . . . a great dancer and all that . . . but it's you I want to spend a bit of time with.'

'Ohh!' Abbie breathed softly, her

heart now beating even faster.

'Anyway, I don't want to come between you and your friend, so I've decided to take the opportunity to check out a few new short-break locations. It's only for a few days. I'll be back at the beginning of next week.'

Though disappointed that she wouldn't see Tim for a few days, in another way, Abigail was relieved.

It postponed the next time she and Jenny would be vying for Tim's attention and, more immediately, it gave her and Jenny the opportunity to settle into the morning appointments without any conflicting tension between them.

'Thanks for telling me. Have a great time!'

Did Tim detect the wistful note in her voice?

Whatever, he said softly, 'I wish you were coming with me! Another time, eh?'

'Yes ... perhaps!' not ready to commit herself.

She put the phone down, unaware of her rosy cheeks.

'Who was that? You look like the cat who's got the cream!' Jenny asked, coming to the desk to check the appointments book, leaving her previous client to enjoy her post-massage relaxation.

'Tim. He's going away for a few days.'

Jenny glanced at her, her eyebrows raised. 'You don't look too upset?'

'No, well, he murmured a few 'sweet nothings'!'

'Did he?'

Jenny seemed momentarily disconcerted but then she shrugged and said with a grin, 'Good on you, kid! Now, where's my next client? Isn't she here yet?

'There's a Mrs Gaskell down here, due for a pedicure at ten o'clock, followed by a Mrs Ramsden at half-past.'

Abbie was immediately concerned. 'Oh, no! Not another!'

'Another what?'

'Missed appointment. There were a few the day you came.'

'It happens.'

'Yes, but it's bad for business. Why can't they phone to cancel?'

Neither lady appeared and the two girls spent the half-hour wiping down all the surfaces . . . then at twenty-five to eleven both ladies arrived together.

'Sorry we're a bit late!' Mrs Gaskell apologised. 'My son rang just as I was setting out. He lives in Malaysia, so I couldn't put him off.'

'That's all right,' Abigail murmured, thinking that thirty-five minutes was hardly 'a bit' late. She forced a smile and said, 'You're here now and I've got a colleague helping out, so we can do you both together.'

Since the two ladies were friends, there was a lot of teasing and laughter as their feet were bared and the time passed with much hilarity. Both ladies made appointments for in a month's time and promised to recommend the salon to their other friends.

The same happened with the eleven o'clock appointment . . . except that the client arrived at twenty-past just in front of the eleven-thirty client. This lady didn't apologise for her lateness, but breezed in as though she had all the time in the world.

When three clients turned up for the same appointment at half-past one, one of them being one of Monday's non-arrivals, Abbie began to suspect that the 'trickster' was at work again.

A few well-phrased questions confirmed her suspicions. Yes, the appointments had been changed over the telephone. No, they didn't notice any particular accent of the caller. They had simply assumed that it was Abigail.

The question was, who was it? Who had had access to her appointment book? It had been open and available for all to see on the opening day. Even after that, any number of people could have seen it . . . anyone who arrived for an appointment and sat in the reception area awaiting their turn.

Her eyes narrowed. Or, anyone turning up on spec with a broken fingernail! A convenient scapegoat, she thought, shaking her head at her too-ready thought. Why would Corinda bother whether she made a success of her business or not?

It was a frustrating problem that showed no signs of dying away. But, what had she to go on? Nothing! All she could do was try to sort out the problem before she had too many disgruntled clients on her hands.

It wasn't until later in the day that Abigail remembered that she hadn't mentioned the possible intruder from the flat upstairs to Tim when he had phoned earlier.

It was too late now and would have to wait until Tim returned. Meanwhile, she would have to keep extra vigilant.

The officer at the local police station hadn't shown too much concern over the new note. It didn't actually threaten her and, whilst he agreed that it made her uneasy, all he could suggest was that she made sure she locked the door securely each night and he would instruct any patrolling police cars to keep a lookout each time they passed by.

The extra work involved in squeezing in the missed appointments, made both girls tired by the end of the day and Jenny looked especially washed out. The rescheduling of appointments over next few days kept their workload at a premium and seemed to cause an undercurrent of tension. Jenny seemed a little subdued, Abigail thought.

'Aren't you feeling well?' Abbie asked in concern.

'I'm all right!' Jenny snapped. 'Stop fussing! It's as bad as living with my mother!'

'You look tired, that's all I'm saying. You've not been well since that last 'take-away' we had. D'you think I'd better let them know, in case there's any others who've been affected?'

'No, don't do that! I'm all right. All

you care about is running this place! Isn't my work good enough for you?'

'Yes, of course it is. You've worked very hard this week. I'm grateful. I don't know how I would have managed without you. What do you plan to do next week?'

'I can stay a bit longer,' Jenny offered. 'In fact I'm wondering whether or not to hand in my notice. I could work here full-time then, couldn't I?'

Abigail hesitated. 'I'd love you to work here, Jenny, I just feel you need to find your own flat. We're a bit cramped for space for a permanent arrangement. I'm not sure we'd still be on speaking terms if we lived together like this for too long!'

'That flat upstairs is going to be yours, isn't it?'

'Yes ... but not for another two months or so. As yet, it has nothing to do with me.'

'I can't see why the former tenant shouldn't just put her things in storage. That's what most people would do.'

'Possibly . . . but her lease was extended before I took over the shop. Don't let's fall out about it. Maybe you should give in your notice at the end of this week if you still feel you'd like to work here permanently . . . and, while you're working your notice, I could employ a student from the college on Work Experience.

'By then, we might know when Mrs Crompton is going to be ready to move out. You could put a 'wanted' notice in the newsagent's window. I could even put a notice up in here. One of our clients might know of somewhere appropriate, mightn't they?'

'Would you really do that?' Jenny seemed touched by the notion.

'Of course I would! You're good at the job, Jenny. I know you can do everything as well as I can. I'll find it hard to manage without you now.'

'Is it all right if I go Friday night? I've got things to sort out before I see Miss Speight I've looked in the diary and we're only half-booked for Saturday.'

Abbie agreed and that was what happened. On Friday evening, she closed the salon as soon as the last client had left and, half an hour later, bade farewell to Jenny. Her flat felt strangely empty, in spite of it having been cramped with the two of them in it. She felt very much at a loose end and, on an impulse, went to the flower shop next door to see what the girls had planned for the evening.

'Come bowling with us,' Liz offered. 'We'll have a good laugh. There's usually about eight of us turn up . . . and we have a cheap meal afterwards.'

Abigail agreed and enjoyed the evening tremendously. It made her feel that she was more settled in the village and beginning to build a new life for herself.

Saturday's appointments flowed one after the other. At half past three she closed the door after the last client of the day, thankful that she hadn't booked any later appointments. She was looking forward to a shower and putting her feet up . . . and maybe read a book later.

'Mmm!' She sighed in contentment as she closed the appointment diary. Her flat was her own again and life was looking bright.

A man's figure approaching the salon from his parked car caught her attention. Startled, she did a double take.

Oh, no! She thought she had seen the last of him!

It was her ex-boyfriend, Jonathan Routledge.

7

Her breath caught in her throat. Now, what was he doing here? Surely he hadn't misunderstood their last meeting together when she had told him exactly what she thought of his two-timing act!

She contemplated locking the door in his face and ignoring him . . . but didn't want to risk causing a scene outside the salon.

She opened the door before he had the chance to open it himself and faced him boldly. 'Jonathan! To what do I owe the pleasure?'

'Abigail!' He irritatingly imitated her tone of voice. 'What a nice welcome!'

'I don't know how you've got the nerve to come here! I told you when we last spoke together that I didn't want to see you again . . . ever . . . and nothing has changed my mind!' She faced him furiously, hands on hips.

'May I come in . . . please?' he added belatedly.

'Why?'

'Because I don't want to stand on your doorstep. And, to deflate your ego, it isn't you whom I've come to see!'

She felt like shutting the door in his face but curiosity made her resist the temptation.

'Oh? Well, there's no-one else here!'

Jonathan looked surprised. 'I was told I'd find Jenny here.'

'Jenny? Why?'

'I need to see her. Has she been here?'

'Well, yes . . . she's been here for a week . . . but she left yesterday. Why do you want to see her?' She was beginning to feel alarmed. Why should Jonathan want to see Jenny? She wasn't aware that they had met more than fleetingly. Had he some bad news for her . . . from her family or someone?

'I'd much rather have this conversation inside,' Jonathan insisted.

With bad grace, Abigail stepped aside

and invited him in, determined he would go no further than the reception area. 'I hope you're going to keep this short!'

'Where's Jenny gone?'

'What business is that of yours?'

'Look, Abigail, I know you think I treated you badly, but don't make this any harder than it is for me! I want to see her. Isn't that enough?'

'No, Jonathan. It isn't! I wouldn't introduce you to my worst enemy, never mind one of my friends! All I will say is that she has gone back to Bolton. Apart from that, I don't know where she is. She's probably gone back to the flat she is sharing with Carol. I didn't actually ask where she was going to stay.'

'I've been there. Carol hasn't heard from her.'

'Well, she only left yesterday. Maybe she went somewhere else first. She said she had something else to sort out before she goes in to see Miss Speight to hand in her notice at the salon. I assume she's doing that on Monday.'

'She doesn't need to hand in her notice! She quit two weeks ago. Didn't you know?'

Abigail was astounded. 'Are you sure? Surely she would have told me!' Why had Jenny deceived her.

Jonathan's voice cut across her thoughts. 'There's something else she obviously hasn't told you.'

'What's that?'

'She's pregnant.'

'Who's the father supposed to be?'

Jonathan adjusted his tie and looked embarrassed. 'I am.'

Abigail took a step backwards in shock. 'You?'

'Sorry, Abigail. I know that disillusions your faith in me . . . but, yes. It's me.'

Abigail's brain whizzed round doing rapid calculations. Her eyes narrowed as the truth hit her. 'Does that mean that, whilst you were two-timing Fay with me, you were also two-timing both of us with Jenny?'

Jonathan sighed in exasperation. 'All

right, Abigail. I know I deserve a worse fate than death . . . but I do like Jenny.'

'Like? Shouldn't that be 'love'?'

'All right! I love her! Will that do?'

'It makes it better. Poor Jenny. No wonder she's been a bit ratty over the past few days!' And making a play for Tim! A sudden suspicion hit her. 'Had she told you she was pregnant before she came here?'

'Well, yes. She told me almost as soon as she knew. It shook me rather, I can tell you! Me? A father?'

'She must be feeling very unhappy . . . and very lonely.' A thought having crossed her mind, she asked. 'What are your intentions when you find her?'

'I'll ask her to marry me. I know you despise me, Abigail.' He clasped her arms just above her elbows and looked down at her. 'Maybe with just cause? But I do love her. She's the first girlfriend I've ever said that about!'

'Then go and tell her so!'

'Where will she have gone?'

'She's probably gone home to her parents' house. They live in Blackburn. If you hang on just a minute, I'll get you her address.'

Abbie spent Saturday evening with Liz and Margot. They went to the cinema and had a few drinks afterwards and back home by eleven o'clock. She wondered how soon Tim would be back from his short-breaks excursion.

At least he hadn't taken Corinda with him, Abbie having noticed her a few times, busy in the Travel office.

She rose early on Sunday morning and heeded the call of the parish church bells summoning worshippers to church. It seemed as though a lot had happened since the previous Sunday. Was it really only a week since she and Tim had gone to Southport and discovered their liking for each other? It seemed far longer.

Jonathan was parked outside her premises on her return from church. He had come to collect Jenny's belongings, he said.

'So, it all turned out well between you, did it?' Abigail asked as she unlocked the door.

'Yes. I'm sorry it took me so long to come to terms with the coming baby,' Jonathan confessed. 'I couldn't take it in and just felt I was being trapped. Once I had had the chance to think about it, I knew it was only hastening on what would have happened anyway. I really do love Jenny and won't ever do anything to hurt her.'

'Good! You'll have me to deal with if you do!' Abigail threatened in a jocular manner.

She held out her hand, intending only to shake his hand in a semi-formal farewell but Jonathan ignored her hand and clasped her around the waist, lifting her feet from the ground and swinging her around in sudden exuberance. He grinned disarmingly.

'I'm grateful for your friendship, Abbie . . . and no hard feelings, eh?'

Abigail smiled back. 'No hard feelings,' she agreed. 'Do you want a coffee or something while I get Jenny's things together?'

'No, if it's all right, I'll head straight back. I'm taking Jenny to meet my parents this afternoon. I'll pop along to the newsagents to get a Sunday paper while I'm waiting. Do you want one, too?'

'Yes, please, I'll have The Telegraph, if they have one left.'

Jonathan light-heartedly dropped a kiss on her lips as he turned to go, then picked her up around her waist and spun her round, laughing at her squeals to put her down.

Across the road, Tim, looking for a space to park his car, saw a man come out of Abbie's salon and was momentarily stunned by the exuberance of their parting. At first he thought that maybe her twin brother was back — but, no, this man was far too dark.

He'd had a good break and was now hoping to resume his friendship with Abbie. Hopefully, with Jenny now returned home.

He parked his car and retraced his steps to the main road, deciding to stop in the newsagents for a Sunday paper. He arrived just in time to hear the female assistant say, 'You look happy!' as she took payment for the newspapers from the man at the counter. 'Won the lottery, have you?'

'Better than that!' the man announced, smiling broadly at the other customers. 'I'm getting married! And we're having a baby!' He included Tim in his wide grin.

With a sense of renewed shock, Tim recognised the man as being the one who he had just seen leaving Abigail's salon ... and whom he had just witnessed swinging her off her feet and twirling her around. No wonder he was feeling so happy!

'Congratulations,' he said tonelessly as he turned to pay for his paper, his heart churning.

Tim frowned as he watched Jonathan turn to the left and, presumably, return to Abbie's Beauty Salon again. To his

119

utter dismay, he felt well and truly deflated.

He was still frowning as he left the shop. He glanced towards the beauty salon, wondering if he should knock on the door and get his best wishes over and done with.

No! He could see that Abigail's fiancé's car was still there . . . and he felt too raw to expose himself to their obvious love for each other. With his face set sternly, he unlocked the door leading up to his flat and went up the stairs.

Abigail moped around the small flat after Jonathan had gone. She felt restless. She was longing to see Tim again. She had missed him all week and now that Jenny was settled with Jonathan, there wouldn't be any complications getting in the way of their budding friendship.

She made herself a mug of coffee. She sipped it slowly, glancing at the front-page articles in the local newspaper about a local man who had escaped from prison. By the time she had re-read the leading item three times and still didn't know what it was about, she put it down with a sigh, feeling at a loss what to do for the remainder of the day.

The events of the past thirty-six hours had taken an emotional toll on her, leaving her feeling to keyed up to just sit around. What if she asked Tim out for lunch? That would brighten things up and give them both the opportunity to get to know each other a bit better.

She quickly stepped outside and went to his open porch to ring the bell to his flat. A few seconds elapsed . . . then Tim's voice came through the 'intercom' grill.

'Hello? Can I help you?'

'Tim! It's Abigail. I'm glad you're back. I was wondering if you would like to have lunch with me somewhere? Unless you've got something else planned, that is.' She waited hopefully.

Again, a few seconds went by. Then, 'I'm sorry, Abigail. I'm deep in the

throes of unpacking my things and I
don't really want to break off.'

'Oh!' She paused, not understanding
the coolness in his voice. 'I could make
sandwiches and come up and help you,'
she suggested hesitantly, not wanting to
be put off too readily.

'I don't think that's a good idea,
Abigail. Do you? I'm sure you've got
lots of other things to be doing . . . '

She felt the pain of his rejection.
'Well, I . . . '

' . . . with the coming wedding and
all that.'

Wedding? How . . . ?

'Oh!'

Her fingers touched the side of her
face as his meaning sank in.

'Did you meet Jonathan? Did he tell
you?'

She felt depressed and flattened by
his reaction. He must have felt more
towards Jenny than either of them had
realised! He sounded as though he had
been hurt by the news.

'I would hardly say we had met

. . . but, yes, he was announcing the good news to all within hearing in the newsagents! I must admit, it took me by surprise. I must offer my congratulations!'

Since his voice sounded anything but happy, Abigail knew his words were far from the truth.

'Yes. It took me by surprise, as well.' Abigail tried to keep her voice bright, though she felt her heart was breaking. 'Still, it's all ending happily and that's the main thing, isn't it?'

'If you say so. He's gone, then, has he?'

'Yes.'

There was a heavy silence. Abigail bit her lower lip. Tim sounded hurt . . . and so was she! Pity they couldn't help each other! Her throat felt tight.

Fighting back tears, she rushed back into her salon feeling totally rejected and miserable. After Jonathan's betrayal she had vowed never to let a man demoralise her again.

As soon as Abigail wakened on

Monday morning, she instinctively knew that something was amiss . . . though she didn't know what. She lay still for a moment, remembering that she was now alone in the flat . . . but it wasn't Jenny's absence that was different. She could hear water running!

Oh, no! Had she left the tap running last night? Surely not!

She swung her legs out of her sleeping bag and on to the floor . . . straight into freezing cold water! She pulled her feet upwards and stared in dismay at her carpet. It was at least two inches deep in water!

Her slippers were bobbing drunkenly in front of her, not quite decided whether to sink or swim! Either way, they were saturated! She sighed resignedly. Sitting here looking at it wouldn't help to get whatever it was fixed! She carefully stepped back into the water and plodded through to her small bathroom.

Water was bubbling out from behind the washbasin. Crouching down to look at it more closely, she could see that it was leaking out of a joint in the pipe. Now what?

She turned the cold-water tap on, which immediately lessened the flow from the pipe. That was a help . . . but more water was still seeping out on to the floor. She needed to find the stopcock. It wasn't there . . . so it must be under the sink in the main room.

She rushed over and yanked open the door, hastily pulling out the contents of the cupboard. There it was! She reached in and turned it until it stopped. Had that done the trick?

She splashed back through the water to the bathroom, heaving a sign of relief as she saw that the bubbling water had ceased. At least it wouldn't get any worse now! But what was she to do?

Her carpets were sodden, along with all items that had stood on the floor — and what about the salon?

She hurried over to the communicating door. Oh, no! It was obvious at once that water had seeped through. It had

had all night to do so! This was all she needed!

She thrust a hand back through her hair. Where to start? She needed a plumber and then had to get her carpets dried out. It wasn't going to happen before her first client was due! Her heart sank. More cancellations!

Disconsolately, she turned away. She had better get dressed and then get on the phone.

Fortunately, she had kept the card of the plumber who had installed the shower and left a message on his answer-phone.

Using towels to soak up the water, she set about the task, filling bowl after bowl of wrung-out water. There seemed no end to it. There was no way she was going to be able to dry everything out today!

Probably not even in a couple of days! She stood up, easing her back and looking disconsolately at her living-room. For the time being, it was uninhabitable.

She looked up at the ceiling, seeing not the ceiling but the flat above it. Was it possible?

Just for a night or two? Could Tim advise her? Would he, was probably the more relevant question.

She hesitated.

She genuinely needed help . . . and she was sure he would give it . . . but it wasn't going to be easy to ask!

8

As Abigail made her way forwards into the salon, she saw Tim emerge from his premises and cross the pavement towards his car, now parked in its usual place. If she wasn't quick, she was going to miss him! She hurriedly pulled back the bolts on the door and rushed outside.

'Tim!' she called. 'I know you're a bit upset with me . . . but I need your help . . . or, at least, your advice.'

He halted in surprise and she could see concern in his eyes as he looked at her. 'Abigail! Are you all right?'

'Yes . . . but my bedsit isn't!'

'What's happened? There haven't been any more incidents, have there?'

'No. At least, not, I think, created by anyone deliberately! No, a water pipe has burst and there are a couple of inches of water on the floor. It's flooded!'

She took a deep breath, hating to have to ask him . . . but she couldn't think of any viable alternative. 'Do you think I could possibly camp out in Mrs Crompton's flat for a few days?'

'I'm not sure I'm the one to help you, there.' Tim glanced at his watch. 'Look, I can give you five minutes. Let me come and see what's happening.' He stepped past her into the salon. 'Whew! I see what you mean! Do you know where it's coming from? You'll have to turn the main tap off.'

'I've done that. And I've left a message with a plumber . . . but it's even worse in my bedsit, look!' She threw open the door. 'I can't live in here until it's dried out . . . and I want to start with the salon. I've had to cancel today's clients but it's not good for business.' She spread her hands helplessly. 'I just thought, if I could live in the flat this week, it would give me time and space to get sorted.'

'Knowing Mrs Crompton, I'm sure she won't mind,' Tim said, 'but, it's really not up to me. Your friend, Colin Jackson, is her agent. You'll have to ask him and get him to sort out any rent, or whatever. And use his keys. Mrs Crompton left a key with me as a safety precaution. I can't just hand it over, not without asking her.'

Abigail swallowed hard. He wasn't prepared to help her, then. Still, as he had said, it wasn't really his place to.

'No, of course not. I'm sorry to have bothered you. I'll ring Colin, then,' she said, holding open the door for him to leave. 'Thanks for the advice.'

'If you need any help clearing up I can give you the number of my cleaner,' he said as he left.

She looked at him. Tim's eyes were sympathetic. Her heart flipped. He wasn't entirely unmoved by her then. If only she could give him time, maybe he could grow to care for her?

'No, thanks. I'll manage. It will give me something to do! Thanks for offering.'

'Glad to be of assistance! Sorry if I

sounded a bit churlish yesterday. It was a mixture of surprise and, well, you know, disappointment at how things have turned out.'

Abigail nodded wryly. 'Yes. I know. I understand.' She was glad they had had this chance to talk. It would make things easier next time they met . . . and, who knows, they might get together, even yet?

She got on the phone to Colin as soon as Tim had gone and he said he would see what he could arrange for her. The plumber returned her call and promised to drop by within half an hour to size up the job and make sure she had turned off the water correctly . . . but he couldn't come to do the work until tomorrow at the earliest. 'You can try someone else, if you want to,' he offered, 'but I don't think you'll get anyone to come out straightaway.'

'I'll go through the Yellow Pages and see what's what . . . and get back to you if necessary.'

Over half-an-hour later, she phoned

him back. 'You were right,' she told him. 'I'll look forward to seeing you as soon as you can come.'

She then set about scooping up more water. It was back-breaking work and she was glad when Joe, the plumber, arrived. It gave her a good excuse to stop for a while.

When he had made sure everything was secure, he repeated his promise to return as soon as possible and bade her goodbye. Abigail decided to go next door to see Wendy and the other girls in the flower shop and bemoan her bad luck.

A mug of coffee later and accompanied by offers to help in their lunch hour, Abigail returned to her work.

Colin was soon on the phone. He'd talked to the senior manager and they had agreed that, under the circumstances, they would draw up a short tenancy agreement and allow her to move upstairs straightaway.

'I'll have to come round to make a quick inventory of Mrs Crompton's belongings,' he added, 'but I can't see it being a problem. See you soon.'

He came an hour later and they went upstairs together. It seemed just as she had seen it with Tim a couple of weeks ago.

Colin read the meter for the gas and electricity and glanced generally at the cupboards.

'We'll have to trust you on this,' he said. 'Just use the bare minimum. Where will you sleep? In Mrs Boardman's bed? Have you got your own bedding?'

'No. I'll sleep in my sleeping bag on the sofa,' she decided. 'It will be simpler that way. Thanks for your help, Colin.'

It was with a lighter heart that she returned downstairs to gather together some things to take up to the flat. She wouldn't need much; just her clothes and a few personal items and a bit of food.

★ ★ ★

Tim had a busy day. He had to write descriptions of the holiday venues he had visited on the west coast of France and compile a new brochure for them. He had every confidence that the resorts would sell well.

He couldn't help feeling disappointed that he wouldn't now be taking Abigail with him when he made any follow-up visits. She had very much been in his mind when he had been looking them over, imaging her delight at the long beaches of silvery sand with the Atlantic waves crashing on to them; the busy fishing ports and market towns; and the almost Mediterranean climate that the area enjoyed.

He was aware of Abbie's presence next door, could hear her voice faintly talking to the plumber when he came; and, later, saw Colin Jackson arrive and presumably take Abbie up to see Mrs Crompton's flat.

He was surprised at his concern for her, having decided not to think tenderly of her any more, since there was now no chance of them pursuing their promising friendship . . . but he supposed it must be impossible to suddenly extinguish such feelings.

He hadn't expected it to hit him like this. He had really felt they had something going for them. He had begun to think of her in terms of permanence . . . that they would have the rest of their lives to find out everything there was to discover about each other . . . and it came as a shock to him to suddenly realise that he had imagined himself married to her and that they had children playing on those lovely beaches.

With a sudden swift movement he closed his programme, switched off his computer and stood up.

'Hold the fort, Corinda, will you? I'm going out.'

'Oh? is anything the matter?'

'No, of course not! I . . . I just need to go to town. I'll be back before closing time. If there are any problems, just give me a call.'

True to his word, he returned just after five o'clock and could see one of the girls from the flower shop pushing round some sort of cleaning machine in Abbie's salon. He was glad she had some friends to help her.

Later, after he had eaten at the Golden Lion, he thought of his earlier attitude to Abbie when she had asked about moving into Mrs Crompton's flat. He had been a bit hard on her; he could have said it was all right — Mrs Crompton would have trusted his judgement.

In fact, he had meant to visit her again long before this, especially since Abigail had thought she had heard noises up there.

Probably creaking boards or some such occurrence. It happened in properties the age of these.

Stirred by his conscience, he made the snap decision to visit the elderly lady that same evening. It would be better than moping about his flat, wishing he were still on holiday, his dreams of Abigail still intact.

He bought a box of chocolates and a bunch of flowers and drove the ten miles or so to Ormskirk General Hospital. There she was, at the far end of the ward. That was a good sign . . . she must be nearly ready to go home. He smiled at the other ladies as he passed them, responding light-heartedly to their banter.

Mrs Crompton welcomed him with a smile, her eyes lighting up at the sight of the chocolates. 'Eeh, you shouldn't have, love . . . but thanks all the same. Let's open them now, shall we?'

He laughed at her eagerness and slit open the cellophane wrapper, watching as her hand hovered over the array of chocolates before pouncing on the coffee cream.

'Now, why does that not surprise me?' he laughed.

'Go on with you! You know me too well!' she said as she popped the chocolate into her mouth and sighed with delight. 'So, let's be having all the gossip, lad. Who's been doing what? Any births, marriages or deaths?'

He winced over the first two but decided not to go along that line. He told her about Abbie starting her salon, brought in the girls at the flower shop, whom she knew quite well, told her about his sojourn in France and wondered how he could ask her about who else had a key to her flat without unnecessarily alarming her.

As it happened, he didn't need to. Mrs Crompton suddenly said, 'I had an unexpected visitor a week or so back. That nephew of mine . . . well, great nephew, really . . . you know the one. Daniel, his name is; never done a day's work in his life! I thought, 'Eh up, what's he after?' Before I knew what he was doing, he had my locker open and was rooting through my handbag, the cheeky so-an-so. Said he wanted a ciggy but he knows I don't smoke. Anyway, I gave him a tenner and put my bag safely out of his reach and he left soon afterwards.'

She leaned forward and took hold of his hand. 'I've been hoping as how you'd come to see me, Tim, because, although I can't be sure he took it, I haven't been able to find the key to my door since . . . and I know I must have had it in my bag because, otherwise, how could I have locked my door when I left? My door is locked, isn't it? You'd have noticed if it wasn't, wouldn't you?'

Tim patted her hand. 'Yes, it's locked, Mrs Crompton, and I've got your spare key safe . . . and, of course, the estate agent has another key. Now, that brings me to a little problem that arose last night.'

He proceeded to tell her about the run of bad luck that Abigail had had and lastly, about the water pipe bursting and Abbie needing somewhere to sleep until she could get everywhere dried out. He didn't tell her about the suspicious sounds Abigail had heard . . . but it now seemed likely that the nephew had indeed been in the flat on occasions, possibly stealing things to sell . . . and he didn't like the idea that Abigail was now living there on her own.

'I tell you what I'll do, Mrs Crompton. First thing tomorrow morning, I'll get on to a locksmith and get your locks changed . . . the front one and the one upstairs. How about that? That will put your mind at rest . . . and mine, too.'

Abbie wasn't sure what had wakened her. It was still dark, but she guessed it was just before dawn. She just knew that someone else was in the flat. She froze, holding her breath. Whoever it was, was creeping over to the window. Was it only one person? Or could she detect two?

A female voice hissed, 'What are you doing?' answering her question. There were two!

'Just checking that the curtains are closed.' The male voice spoke quietly but in total control. 'There's no need to whisper. No-one is here.'

Abigail held her breath . . . and, with

a blinding flash, the light came on. She clutched the top of her sleeping bag up to her chin, her eyes wide with fright.

The intruders looked equally startled. The girl, dressed in black leathers, was obviously the person she had seen . . . was it a week ago? But it was the man who alarmed her the most. He, too, was dressed completely in black, with a balaclava over his head. Only his eyes were showing.

9

'Who on earth are you?' the man demanded harshly, moving towards the sofa. Abigail screamed and tried to scramble out of her sleeping bag. She wasn't sure what she was intending to do. She just wanted to put more distance between herself and the approaching figure.

He moved swiftly and had grabbed hold of her arms just above her elbows before she could get her feet free of her sleeping bag. Shaking her roughly, he dragged her off the sofa and hauled her to her feet.

'I asked you a question!'

'I . . . I live downstairs . . . in the beauty salon . . . but the floor's flooded,' Abigail stammered. 'C . . . Colin, the agent said I could sleep up here until I've got it sorted.'

'Beauty salon! Huh! Some people

have more money than sense!' The man thrust her back on to the sofa.

'What's going on? What are you doing here?' Abigail looked from the man to the girl. She seemed to be about her own age. She had long blonde hair and heavily made-up eyes, giving her a hard appearance. She couldn't expect much help there!

'W . . . Why have you broken in, like this?'

'We didn't break in! We have a key!' He waggled it in front of her face.

At least the light in his eyes changed from threatening to amusement. He wasn't totally bad, then.

'Oh! Do you know Mrs Crompton? Has she said you can stay in her flat?' she asked, hoping to hold on to some sort of control of the situation.

She tried to smile as she reached for her clothes that she had left hanging over the back of a chair but knew her attempt wouldn't win her any prizes.

'What do you think?' The girl sneered. 'You don't look the stupid

143

kind.' She turned to the man. 'What are we going to do with her, Dan?'

'I don't know yet . . . but we can't have her free to roam around. Go into the bedroom with her and watch her while she gets dressed. Don't let her try anything.' He began to prowl around the room, poking about in the partly packed boxes. 'Hey, you, whatever you're called! What's all this in aid of?'

Abigail tried hard to control her fast beating heart. She halted in the bedroom doorway.

'Mrs Crompton is moving out as soon as she comes out of hospital.' She was surprised how normal her voice sounded. Inside she was quaking. 'She's got somewhere else lined up. Tim has been helping her to pack her things.'

'Tim who?'

'J . . . Just a neighbour.'

'Likely to come back, is he?'

Abigail's mind whirled. Would it help her if the man thought someone might be calling? Or would it make him more desperate? 'I don't know. He didn't say.'

She was conscious of the weight of her mobile phone in her trouser pocket. When she was wearing her trousers its tell-tale bulge would show. She needed to get rid of it somewhere where she could get to it later. If she could manage to make a quick call to someone . . . or better still, send a text message . . .

How desperate were the couple? And what did they have to do with Mrs Crompton? How had they got hold of her key? The memory of something Tim had said, a 'ne'er-do-well' nephew,' sprang to mind. Was that who he was? Not very desperate then, she hoped! Except, why the balaclava?

'Can I get dressed now?' she asked, principally to get away from the man's horrid gleaming eyes. They were the most unnerving part of the situation.

'Yeah, and no tricks! Leave the door open, Bev. And keep a close watch on her! I don't trust her!'

Bev gave her a push. 'You heard what he said . . . and I'm right behind you! So watch it!'

Abigail laid her clothes on the bed as Bev switched on the light. 'Damn!' Bev had realised that the curtains were open.

As Bev rushed across the room, Abigail slid her mobile phone out of her trouser pocket and slipped it under the pillow. She might have the opportunity to reclaim it later.

'Hurry up! I want you back out there!' Bev snapped.

'Have you known him long?' Abigail asked, as she pulled on her light sweater, hoping to melt her coolness. And, she was conscious that this room probably adjoined with Tim's bedroom. Was it possible he might hear their voices?

'Button it! It's none of your business!'

'Sorry! I was only making conversation.'

'Don't bother! We'll tell you all we want you to know . . . and that won't be very much!'

Abigail concentrated on dressing and was soon ushered back into the living-room. The man, Dan, his name seemed to be, had tipped the contents of her bag on to the table and was rifling through them. 'Where's your mobile phone?' he asked.

Abigail shrugged. 'I haven't one.'

'Everyone in business has a mobile phone these days. What've you done with it?'

She thought quickly. 'I use the one in the salon. I can claim tax relief on it.'

'Hmm. Search her pockets, Bev.'

Bev ran her hands over Abigail's body, but didn't find anything. Dan shrugged, accepting its absence. 'I'm going to have to tie you up,' he informed her, picking up a scarf from amongst the contents of her bag. 'Turn her around, Bev!'

'I need to use the bathroom,' Abbie protested, not entirely untruthfully. She wanted to delay being tied up.

'Go with her!' Dan ordered Bev.

As a delaying tactic, it wasn't very

effective. Bev followed her into the bathroom and lounged against the wall while Abbie cleaned her teeth. When she looked pointedly at the toilet, Bev merely shrugged.

Abbie had hoped for the opportunity to bang on the shared wall with the flat over the flower shop. She wasn't sure which room it co-joined with, but there was a chance that Liz might hear it. But perhaps it was as well she didn't have the opportunity.

Once back in the living-room, Bev roughly pushed her round and held her arms together while Dan tied her scarf around her wrists and another round her mouth. Abigail didn't see the point of resisting. There was no way she could move fast enough to get out of the flat. It would be best to lull them into thinking she accepted her captivity.

She was pushed on to the sofa, where she landed awkwardly. Dan thrust his head close to her face. 'And don't even think of making any noises! I'm a light sleeper!'

The room was plunged into darkness once more and Abigail tried to get into a more comfortable position. How long would they keep her like this? How long were they staying?

She had no means of finding the answers . . . and she did her best to fall asleep.

She must have dozed because suddenly it was much lighter and Bev was moving quietly over to the window, presumably to peep outside.

Abbie made a grunting sound to attract her attention. Her muscles felt on fire and she needed the toilet.

Bev came and looked down at her, obviously understanding her predicament. 'You'll have to wait until Dan's got washed.'

When he came into the living-room, he made no objection to Bev releasing her bonds, but repeated his warning to her not to make a sound or try to make an escape. Abbie realised it was the first time she seen his face. The fact that he had kept it concealed had given her hope that she would be released without harm. She now hoped that the opposite wasn't the case. She looked away quickly, hoping he hadn't noticed the look of interest in her eyes.

The humiliating procedure in the bathroom was repeated. Abbie wondered if Liz would hear the cistern flushing. It would depend on which room she was in. She knew for certain that the bathroom here wasn't next to Tim's flat.

'How long are you intending to keep me here?' she asked before the gag was replaced around her mouth.

'You'll find out when the time comes!'

'I've had no breakfast.'

'Tough! You won't starve!' He pushed her back on to the sofa and jerked his head towards the far side of the room, indicating that Bev join him there.

Abigail winced as she landed, but she wasn't hurt. She struggled into a sitting position and tried to hear what they were saying. She heard the words,

' . . . change of plan . . . too much of a liability . . . have to make our move tonight.'

'What about . . . ?' Bev's voice asked.

'We'll have to take her with us and dump her somewhere!'

'What! You don't mean . . . ?'

'Not unless I have to. I'm not that stupid! No . . . leave her somewhere . . . chance to get away!'

'I told you we should have gone straight to Ireland.'

'Yeah, well, how was I to know there'd be a girl in here? Anyway, I needed somewhere to hole up while I change my appearance! Go and get it ready for me. I'll use her credit card to order our tickets.'

To Abigail's annoyance, she heard Dan's voice coolly giving her Visa card number as he booked two tickets to Dublin for seven o'clock Wednesday morning, arranging to collect them from the desk.

'Thanks, babe!' he drawled, flicking her Visa card in front of her face. 'I'll hang on to this for a while longer! Why pay when you can get someone else to pay for you?'

'I haven't got much credit on it!'

'Not my problem. By the time the demand comes in, I'll be far away . . . living it up in some exotic place! Whilst you, my dear, if you behave yourself and don't do anything silly, will still be here to pick up the pieces . . . and the bill!'

Abigail decided to ignore his taunt. 'I'd like a cup of coffee!' she demanded.

'Good idea! Bev! Do as the lady says!'

After she had drunk it, Abigail laid back against the cushions, hoping neither of her captors would notice that they hadn't replaced the gag. The morning passed slowly. Although the day was now well advanced, it was dim inside the flat since the curtains were drawn across the windows.

Abigail guessed that it was also raining steadily. There wouldn't be many people out on the main street.

She had cancelled her clients. Would anyone notice her absence and wonder where she was? And what about the plumber? He was due today. What would he do?

Surely she would be missed by Tim? Or, if not by him, then by the girls next door. But what would they do? They would see that downstairs was deserted. They might try to contact her up here. Would they knock . . . or phone?

Even the drawn curtains might alert anyone who thought about it. That wouldn't occur to her captors. The girl had been coming and going with the curtains drawn across the window. Please let all these little clues add up to someone, she prayed.

Dan had disappeared into the bathroom and Bev was doing her nails when, at about eleven o'clock, Abigail heard someone knocking on the downstairs door, followed by a voice she recognised as Liz's calling, 'Abbie! Are you up there, Abbie? Are you all right?'

Bev leapt from her seat and swiftly

clapped her hand over Abigail's mouth. 'Keep it shut, if you know what's good for you!' she hissed.

After a few moments, they heard the flap of the letterbox drop and all went silent again. The phone began to ring.

Dan's voice called out from the bathroom, 'Let it ring!' and, eventually, that too went silent. The phone downstairs in the salon was the next to ring.

'Someone's missing you!' Bev quipped lightly. 'Popular girl, are you?'

Abigail shrugged. 'It's probably a client. I do run a business, you know! You'd do well to be getting away from here before someone breaks the door down!'

'We're not that stupid. They'll all assume you've gone out somewhere. You did say you were flooded out! We'll go when we're ready!'

Abigail reluctantly accepted that she was probably right. Without anything further to go by, no-one would want to risk breaking the door down on a mere sense of unease. She tried to remember exactly what she had told the flower shop girls yesterday. They'd know she intended to be in, if she had said so.

As if in response to her thoughts, she heard someone rattling the downstairs door again and a male voice calling through the letterbox, 'Hello? Anybody there?'

It must be the plumber. With a sudden movement, hoping to let him know she was there, Abigail tried to stand up. She hoped to get as far as the window and to try to drag away one of the curtains but Bev was too quick for her. She leapt on top of her and the two girls crashed to the floor.

Without the use of her arms, Abigail could only lie there winded, while Bev kicked her prone body.

'Ouch!'

'Cut it out, you two!' Dan commanded sharply.

Abigail screwed her head round and wasn't sure what shocked her the most . . . Dan's now brightly bleached hair

. . . or the gun in his hand.

'What's going on?' he demanded harshly.

'There's someone else at the door. A man this time,' Bev hissed. She jerked her head towards Abigail. 'She tried to make a break for it!'

He kicked against her leg. 'D'you want to make me use this? I will if I have to! So you'd better keep still!'

The phone in the flat began to ring again. Dan strode over to it and ripped the connection out of the wall. 'Get your face to the floor!' he snapped at Abigail. 'And keep still!' He moved silently across the room and stood by the window, his back against the wall, peering through the narrow gap between the curtain and the wall.

Abigail heard him draw in his breath sharply.

'What is it?' Bev demanded.

'A man and a couple of girls! They're looking up at the window . . . so keep well away! They can't see anything! They look uncertain . . . the man's shrugging . . . he's going back to his van.' He was silent for a moment. Then, 'They've gone.'

No sooner had they relaxed than they heard the sound of the key in the downstairs lock.

Abigail's heart leapt. That must be Tim! He was using his key. How could she warn him of the danger he would be in?

'Good job you bolted the door!' Bev commented.

'Yeah, but they now know someone is in here!' Dan snapped back. 'Do you normally bolt the door?' he shot at Abbie.

Unsure which would be the best response, Abbie compromised. 'Some-times,' she shrugged.

Bev was starting to panic. 'How are we going to get away?' she demanded, her voice rising sharply.

'We'll go when it's dark . . . like we've planned! Stop worrying! They'll do nothing. They've nothing to go on!'

It seemed he was right. Everything

went quiet again and time passed slowly by.

Bev had made a number of cups of coffee and they had raided the fridge, occasionally holding a cup of water to Abigail's mouth while she gulped some of its contents.

Daniel made her stay lying on the floor the rest of the time. There was no way she would be able to leap up from there if the opportunity arose.

10

Tim was restless. He paced up and down in his office. Unless Abigail was having a long lie-in, something was wrong. The girls were anxious too, although he had tried to calm their fears. Until he had tried his key and had been unable to gain access he had thought she was simply taking advantage of having no work to do and was having a lie-in.

The plumber had admitted he wasn't expected until after lunch and suggested Abbie might have gone elsewhere to spend the night. But her car was parked there in plain view.

'Got a boyfriend, has she?' the plumber had asked.

That stalled Tim for a moment. Had Jonathan driven over and taken her home? No, she would have let someone know — the girls, if not himself.

He picked up the phone and rang the flat number. He frowned. It was neither ringing nor giving the 'engaged' tone. Was it out of order? It had been working all right last time he'd used it. Did Abigail know it was out of order?

What about her mobile phone? Maybe he should try that. She hadn't actually given him the number but it was there on her card.

He made up his mind and tapped out her number on the his mobile. He heard the ringing start and then Abigail's voice speaking her recorded message in her 'voice mail' box. Suddenly, the connection was broken. He tried again. This time, a sing-song voice in his ear blithely informed him that the number he had dialled was unobtainable. He frowned, a distinct feeling of unease wrapped itself around him.

★ ★ ★

Daniel strode out of the bedroom, his face like thunder. 'No mobile phone, eh?' He threw it down on to the floor beside Abigail. 'Guess what I found under the pillow!' He stamped on the phone, crushing its outer casing. 'I don't know what you hoped to gain from hiding it! There's no way you would have been able to make a call!'

Abigail shrugged. 'It was worth a try. You would have done the same!'

He thrust his face close to hers. 'Maybe I would! But it's not a game we're playing! This gun is for real . . . and if it comes to a fight, I'll use it!'

★ ★ ★

'Really, Tim!' Corinda protested. 'Will you sit down and stop pacing the floor like a nervous expectant father!'

She tapped away at her keyboard, the staccato sound of the keys ripping through Tim's tense nerves. 'I don't know why you're bothering about her! I'd have thought you'd be glad to think

161

she has upped and gone!'

'But she hasn't gone!' Tim uncharacteristically snapped. 'She's still in there! I know it! And I don't like it!'

'Well, neither do I! But don't worry, she won't stick it out much longer. I've got a few more tricks up my sleeve! She'll be glad to see the back of the place before you know it!'

Corinda stood up as she spoke and reached out her elegantly manicured hand to trail the back of a finger down his cheek . . . and was totally unprepared when Tim grabbed hold of her wrist, almost causing her to lose balance.

'What do you mean, Corinda? What are you talking about?'

Corinda struggled to free herself from Tim's grip. 'Don't, Tim! You're hurting! I didn't mean anything!'

'Tell me what you meant!'

Corinda laughed nervously. 'Just a few little hints that she wasn't wanted around here. Nothing dangerous, or anything illegal!'

Light dawned in Tim's mind. 'Like breaking the window? Sending anonymous notes? Cancelling her workmen? I can't believe you'd do this!'

'Like I said, just little hints. I thought you'd be pleased to see her go!'

'Pleased! Do I look as if I'm pleased? You must be mad! Or sick!'

'I did it for you!' Corinda wailed. 'For us! I thought . . .'

'There is no 'us', Corinda!'

He shook her shoulders as he spoke, too agitated to take note of the look of alarm on Corinda's face as another thought struck him. 'Good Lord, did you plan this as well, Corinda? Did you somehow sabotage her water supply, making the place uninhabitable?'

'No! How could I? I couldn't get into the place!'

'Huh!' With a look of disgust, she pushed her away from him. 'You'd better be right in that . . . because if you're not . . .'

He left the threat unfinished as he strode out of the travel shop and stared

163

up at the window above the beauty salon, still hoping that he was worrying over nothing. Who was in there? If it were indeed Dan Crompton, why should that put Abigail in danger? Why should he prevent her from leaving, from contacting anyone?

It didn't make sense!

But he felt so helpless! He couldn't get in — and Abigail couldn't get out!

He made a snap decision. He was going to inform the police. If he used his phone, he knew he would get through to Liverpool and he didn't want to make it too official just yet. He was still hoping that he was going to be having a laugh about this in a few minutes' time!

The local bobby, Sergeant Harrison, lived just down the road on the way out of the village. They'd shared a few drinks at times. He was the one to contact.

He was there in a couple of minutes and pleased to find Sergeant Harrison on duty. As nonchalantly as he could, he explained his reasons for concern. It was only when he mentioned Mrs Crompton's name that a look of real interest appeared on the sergeant's face.

'Crompton, eh? The flat over the beauty salon my wife's been going on to me about? There was an incident there a week or so ago, wasn't there? We've been keeping an eye on the place since the window was broken.' He flicked through the report file on the desk, verifying the incident. 'So, the place really belongs to a Mrs Crompton, does it? That's interesting. Hang on a mo!'

He picked up his phone and rapidly dialled a number. 'Sergeant Harrison here, laddie. That man, Crompton, the one wanted for questioning in connection with that attempted bank robbery yesterday? Made any headway on catching up with him yet? No? Well, listen carefully. I've got an idea. You're going to like what I have to tell you!'

Tim felt his blood run cold. Attempted robbery? He'd heard it on the lunchtime news. The security guard had died of his injuries. No name had been given out but obviously the police had some reason to suspect Dan Crompton. Mrs Crompton's great-nephew, whom she'd described as 'ne'er-do-well'!

He whirled around and dashed outside, hearing Sergeant Harrison's voice ringing after him. 'Leave it to the police, Tim!'

Tim raced back through the village but had the sense to park in Leyland Road, round the corner from the row of shops. No sense in alerting the guy. He pondered what he knew of the man. He wasn't a complete fool. Would he come to his senses and give himself up before everything got too far out of hand?

Tim crossed the main road and stood by the old building which housed the estate agency of David Pluck, glancing up at Mrs Crompton's flat. Was he being over imaginative? Or was the wanted man really in there . . . ? And, if so, what had happened to Abigail?

A cold shiver ran through his body.

He stood immobile, this thoughts racing. He was usually quick and assertive with his decisions! Now here he was, dithering about from one thought to another.

However, he couldn't just stand and wait . . . and he had an idea about how to get into the flat. He decided to try to contact Liz again first. She might have heard something to give an indication of what was going on in there . . . and she needed to be warned to keep well out of the way, as did the rest of the shopkeepers — but he'd leave the rest to the police when they got here!

He shook the rain off his head as he waited in the small porch.

Liz's face lit up as she saw him waiting there. 'Tim! Am I glad to see you!'

'Let's get inside and you can tell me what's happened?'

'I'm not totally sure . . . but it seems a bit strange. As you know, we've not seen anything of Abbie all day and the phone in the flat was suddenly cut off whilst we were ringing it.'

'And her mobile!' Tim added. 'Have you heard anything to indicate what might be going on in there?'

'Well, it's been pretty quiet but there have been sounds.'

'Such as?'

'Creaking boards and the toilet flushing.'

'So, they're definitely in there. Look, I've reported it to the police. I'm supposed to be leaving well alone until they get here, but I want to know if Abbie's still safe.'

'They? What d'you mean?' Her hand suddenly shot to her face. 'You don't think it's this nutter who's been sending those anonymous notes, do you?'

Tim's face was grim. He pursed his lips. 'No, not that. Something more like a burglary gone wrong. Someone who knew the flat should be empty and was taken by surprise to find Abigail in there.'

'Are you going to use your key to get in? You will be careful, won't you?'

Tim shook his head. 'I've had a go and the bolts are on. No, I either wait for the police to try to break down the door . . . or I try to get in another way! Through the attic!'

Liz involuntarily looked up at the ceiling. 'Up there?'

'Yours or mine. They're both the same. Let's take a look.'

'Of course. Come on.'

Tim followed Liz up the stairs and studied the layout. The stairway separated the bedrooms and bathrooms of the adjoining properties but he reckoned the two living rooms at the front met on a conjoined wall. Of course! He should have tried listening at his conjoined wall! Too late for that now! He tiptoed over and placed his ear flat against the wall, straining to hear any sound . . . but he couldn't.

'Have you ever been in the attic, Liz?'

'You must be joking! I don't even know how to get in it!'

'The trap door is over the top of the stairs. Have you any steps?'

'Yes. They're in the storeroom down-stairs.'

'Good. What about a torch and something to prise open the wooden cover from above?'

'On the shelf near the steps.'

'Right! Hang on a mo!'

Tim ran lightly down the stairs, found the steps, torch and a strong-looking knife and carried them up to the top of the stairs. He put the torch and knife into the back pocket of his trousers and climbed up the steps until his hands could push against the wooden board. He turned to look at Liz's anxious face.

'Try not to make any noise whilst I'm up there. The sounds might carry. And I'll try not to fall between the rafters! And look out for the police arriving. Tell them I'm up there and won't do anything until they get here. I'm just trying to find out where exactly in the flat they are.'

He carefully lifted the wooden board that served as a cover to the attic to one side and raised his body up through the space. He shone the torch around.

The light from the torch showed the rafters he would have to cross carefully and, at the far side of the attic, he could see there were small spaces at the sides of the brickwork that separated the attics of each property. Could he remove some bricks and squeeze through without making any tell-tale noises?

He balanced his way carefully over. The brickwork was already loose in places. He carefully began to prise an end brick loose . . . and then the next . . . and then the next. The holding cement was past its best . . . he must remember to tell Colin.

He lost track of time but it must have been about half-an-hour before he reckoned it was worth trying to squeeze through the space. Firstly, he took off his jacket and shone the torch through the hole he had made. The next attic seemed identical with the one he was in. The flats were the same way round so the access cover would be very near to the dividing wall. There it was! He could see it!

Gingerly, he began to squeeze his body through the narrow space Bits of loose masonry fell between his feet.

He held his breath. Would the sounds carry? He stayed motionless for a few minutes.

He could hear the rain pelting down on the tiles above him. The wind was getting up, too. It would help to disguise any sounds he made. He felt encouraged to try again. This time, moving slowly and carefully, he man-aged to squeeze and wriggle through the space he had made.

Once through, he straightened care-fully and brushed himself down. It was cold up here! He shrugged himself back into his jacket and, crouching slightly, he carefully stepped over to the dim shape of the access cover.

It wasn't easy to balance and prise up the cover without putting any of his weight on to it, but he could feel the cover moving slightly. He had to do it in absolute silence so as not to betray his presence.

His heart was racing. As soon as he sensed that he could slip his fingers under the lifted edge of the cover, he did so, returning the knife to his back pocket. He crouched as low as he could, putting his ear to the open crack. At first, there was no sound. Then, he heard a man's voice.

'It's time we left! It's raining so hard, there's no-one out there! Get your jacket on. And, you . . .' The tone of his voice changed.

Tim sensed that he was now addressing Abigail, which meant the man had at least one accomplice. ' . . . Any tricks and I'll use this! Tie that other scarf around her mouth, Bev. I can't risk her calling out!'

'You don't have to take me with you. You could leave me here.'

That was Abigail! At least she sounded calm! And probably unhurt, so far!

'What! And risk you setting up an alarm? Not likely! No, you're coming with us . . . until I judge it's safe to dump you!'

'Just do as you're told and you won't get hurt!'

That was a woman's voice. Probably 'Bev', whoever she was. No other voices sounded so he reckoned there were just the two to deal with.

Tim's mind was whirling. Were the police here yet? They might be too late and this pair would get away!

He'd wait until they went downstairs, and then start to follow them and surprise them when they were just outside . . . and hope that Liz had the sense to stay out of sight.

The living room door was opened wider. Holding his breath, Tim peeped through the narrow gap. He could see the top of a woman's head pass beneath him and begin to descend the stairs. Then Abigail's fair head was beneath him.

A dark coat was draped around her

shoulders. Her arms must be tied behind her, he deduced. The man was immediately behind her, one hand gripping her right arm . . . and caught a glimpse of dark metal in his right hand. A gun!

As the figures slowly descended the stairs, Tim carefully eased away the wooden cover and laid it back out of his way. He silently swung himself through the opening and dropped lightly to his feet.

As he did so, everything seemed to happen at once

He saw Dan's head whirl round and his face tighten as he saw him. Making the most of the moment of uncertainty in the man, Tim began to leap down the stairs towards him, realising as he did so that the gun was aimed towards him. He saw Abigail lurch into the man.

Crack!

Tim heard a bullet smack into the wall at the side of him. He continued down the stairs, seeing Dan half braced against the wall, trying to drag Abigail to her feet to hold her in front of him as he backed down the last few stairs.

'Stay where you are or I'll shoot her.' His voice was cold and without emotion.

Bev had opened the door and was screaming to the man to hurry up.

'Let him have it! And her, too!'

She was framed in the doorway. Dan, facing Tim and with Abigail held against his chest, had almost reached her. Dan swung the gun from Abbie's head to point it at Tim.

Tim saw Abigail jerk her knee forwards and then backwards, hooking her foot around the man's leg, sending him off balance as another bullet winged up the stairs, shattering the light bulb on the landing. Bev began to scream uncontrollably.

At the same time, the place was suddenly filled with light from an outside source and a megaphoned voice called out, 'This is the police! We have you covered!'

Dan was momentarily distracted,

half-running towards the direction of the voice.

Tim saw him cringe away from the light and realised he was temporarily dazzled. He launched himself down the few remaining stairs, landing on top of Abigail and Dan and the three of them crashed to the floor at the foot of the stairs.

Tim had the advantage to being on top. His first action was to grab at the wrist of the hand that held the gun. He banged it against the wall, keeping it pointing upwards. 'Drop it! You've no chance!' he shouted.

'Damn you!' Dan spat through his teeth.

Bev's screams had been cut short and uniformed police were already standing over them. A hand reached out and removed the gun from Dan's limp hand.

Tim struggled to his feet and reached down to help Abigail. Her body lay in an awkward position. Her eyes were open and he could see shock in them.

'Are you all right, love? I got here as soon as I could.'

Abigail nodded gratefully. She closed her eyes and swallowed.

One of the policeman helped Tim to lift her to her feet and Tim clasped her in his arms whilst the policeman undid the scarf from around her mouth. The coat had fallen away from her shoulders and the policeman also undid the scarf binding her wrists together. She collapsed against Tim, finding her breath rasping in her throat as tears set in with the reaction to the relief that it was over.

Tim stroked her hair, brushing his lips against her forehead. 'It's all right, darling! It's all right! You're safe now!'

They hardly noticed as Dan Crompton was hauled to his feet, handcuffs snapped on and formally cautioned.

Abigail's wrists were sore and her ankle was painful, having been twisted as she fell. She was thankful of Tim's arms around her. The strength of his body felt good and she felt her sobs easing. Balanced on her left foot, she lifted her head and managed a wobbly smile. 'I'm OK. I just . . . '

'I know, darling! It's all right! I understand.' His arms hugged her close again, almost squeezing the breath out of her.

There was a milling of activity around them. Suddenly Liz was there, adding her arms to the hug and the three of them stood together, each assuring the others that it was over and everything was all right.

A smartly dressed officer laid a hand on Abigail's shoulder. 'We'll need you to come to the police station, miss, and make a statement . . . and you as well, sir. Miss Standish here has already put us in the picture but we need your corroboration.'

Abigail hardly heard him. Her mind had just caught up on some of the words that Tim had spoken to her. She raised her eyes to meet Tim's. 'You said, 'darling' . . . at least twice!' she said softly. 'Does that mean . . . ?'

Tim's shoulders sagged a little as he smiled ruefully. 'I know. I'm sorry. I know you belong to Jonathan and . . . ' His face suddenly looked alarmed. 'I forgot about the baby!' His eyes were full of concern. 'Are you all right? The fall hasn't . . . ?'

Abigail shook her head, partly in bewilderment . . . partly suddenly understanding. 'I'm not pregnant! And I don't belong to Jonathan!'

'You're not? You don't? But Jonathan said . . . '

'He was talking about him and Jenny! It's Jenny who is having a baby . . . and they're getting married at the end of the month.' She smiled sweetly as she placed her hands against his shoulders, looking up at him. 'I don't belong to anybody . . . not yet, anyway!'

Tim smiled down at her, his eyes warming as the tiny crinkle lines at the corners deepened. 'I can think of a way to rectify that! Can you?'

Abigail nodded. 'You've already knocked me off my feet!'

'This time I'll sweep you off your feet permanently, Miss Abigail Norton!'

So saying, he swooped her up into his arms and kissed her firmly on her lips.

THE END

We do hope that you have enjoyed reading this large print book.

Did you know that all of our titles are available for purchase?

We publish a wide range of high quality large print books including:
Romances, Mysteries, Classics
General Fiction
Non Fiction and Westerns

Special interest titles available in large print are:
The Little Oxford Dictionary
Music Book, Song Book
Hymn Book, Service Book

Also available from us courtesy of Oxford University Press:
Young Readers' Dictionary
(large print edition)
Young Readers' Thesaurus
(large print edition)

For further information or a free brochure, please contact us at:
Ulverscroft Large Print Books Ltd.,
The Green, Bradgate Road, Anstey,
Leicester, LE7 7FU, England.
Tel: (00 44) **0116 236 4325**
Fax: (00 44) **0116 234 0205**

Other titles in the
Linford Romance Library:

TOO CLOSE FOR COMFORT

Chrissie Loveday

Emily has shut herself away to work in the family's old holiday cottage in remotest West Cornwall. Her two Jack Russells are all the company she needs . . . until the night she rescues a stranger injured in a raging storm. Cut off by bad weather, and with no telephone, they have to sit it out. Emily begins to warm to Adam. But who is he — and why does he want to stay with her once the storm has passed?

CHRISTMAS CHARADE

Kay Gregory

When Nina Petrov meets charismatic businessman Fenton Hardwick on a transcontinental train to Chicago, she sees him as the solution to her recurring Christmas problem. Every year her matchmaking father produces a different hopelessly unsuitable man for her to marry. Nina decides she needs a temporary fiancé to get him off her case, and Fen seems the perfect candidate for the job — until she makes the mistake of trying to pay him for his help . . .

A LETTER TO MY LOVE

Toni Anders

Devastated when Marcus married someone else, Sorrel resolved to devote her life to her toyshop and her invalid cousin, Alyse. However, when she meets Carl, the Bavarian woodcarver, it provides a romantic distraction — but Marcus's growing friendship with Alyse unsettles Sorrel. She is torn between her still-present love for Marcus, and her cousin's happiness. When Marcus's spiteful sister, Pamela, decides to repossess the toyshop for a wine bar, Sorrel decides to fight them both.

DOCTOR, DOCTOR

Chrissie Loveday

The arrival of a new doctor in a small Cornish hospital causes a stir, especially among the female members of staff. Lauren has worked hard to build her career, along with a protective shell to keep her emotions intact. She won't risk being hurt again, but Tom has other ideas . . . As they share the highs and lows of hospital life, they develop a mutual respect for each other's professional skills — but can there ever be more to their relationship?